MW00778328

Alexander McCall Smith is the author of the bestselling No. 1 Ladies' Detective Agency series. He has written over thirty books for young readers, including three other School Ship *Tobermory* adventures.

Iain McIntosh's illustrations have won awards in the worlds of advertising, design and publishing. He has illustrated many of Alexander McCall Smith's books.

Tobermory

ALEXANDER McCALL SMITH

THE SECRET OF THE DARK WATERFALL

ILLUSTRATIONS BY
IAIN McINTOSH

First published in 2019 by
BC Books,
an imprint of Birlinn Limited
West Newington House
10 Newington Road
Edinburgh
EH9 1QS

www.bcbooksforkids.co.uk

Copyright © 2019 Alexander McCall Smith
Illustrations copyright © 2019 Iain McIntosh

The right of Alexander McCall Smith
to be identified as the author of this work
has been asserted by him in accordance with
Copyright, Designs and Patents Act 1988

All rights reserved.

No part of this publication may be reproduced,
stored or transmitted in any form without the
express written permission of the publisher.

ISBN 978 1 78027 612 0

British Library Cataloguing-in-Publication Data
A catalogue record for this book is available
from the British Library

Typeset by Mark Blackadder

Printed and bound by Clays Ltd, Elcograf S.p.A.

THIS
BOOK
is for
AMALIA

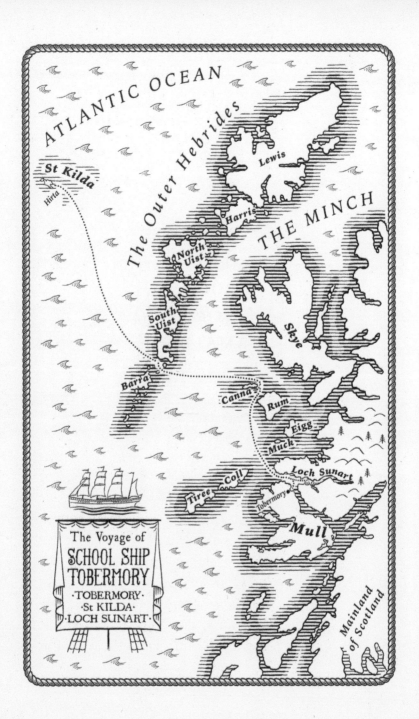

A new term begins

Ben and Fee MacTavish were two ordinary people, rather like you and me. But there was one way in which they were different – they were twins. And it is a bit different being a twin, as any twin will tell you.

"It's like being double," Fee explained. "You feel that you're you, but then you also feel that there's another you – if you see what I mean."

Her brother agreed. "Yes," he said. "It's exactly like that."

There was another way in which their life was not the same as everybody else's. Most people go to ordinary schools – schools that have buildings. These buildings have doors and windows and corridors like any other building and are, of course, always in the same place. When you go to a school like that, you always know exactly where it is going to be. And you would be most surprised if one day you arrived for school and it was not there, but had floated away over

Ben MacTavish

the horizon. Most people would be a bit surprised by that.

But that was exactly what Ben and Fee's school could do. For some time now, they had been students on the School Ship *Tobermory*. This was a large sailing ship based in the town of Tobermory on the Scottish island of Mull. The *Tobermory* took students from all over the world. All the classes were held on board the ship and all the students lived there for several months at a time. Everybody had a cabin, shared with one other person, and this cabin was their bedroom. Three meals a day were served in a large dining hall, called the mess hall, having been cooked in the galley by Cook, a stout man with tattoos of an anchor, a sailing ship and a whale on his arms. The food was always good and, of course, being at sea, the sea air gave everyone a healthy appetite.

Fee and Ben had just celebrated their birthday, which had fallen in the holidays when they were staying with their parents. Their mother and father were both scientists who worked on their own research submarine. Their job required them to go off on long underwater trips, taking samples of seaweed and coral, of sand and rock, and of all the things that make up the underwater world. They also studied fish and sharks, and sometimes even whales, finding out where these wonderful creatures went to, and how they lived their watery lives.

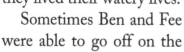

Sometimes Ben and Fee were able to go off on the family submarine, but, for the most part, the need to go to school made that impossible. It was for this reason that they had been enrolled as students on the *Tobermory*.

"We'd love to be able to send you to an ordinary school," said their mother. "But that just wouldn't work, would it? We'd be away on our submarine and you'd have nobody to look after you."

"Don't worry," said Fee. "We much prefer going to ship school anyway, don't we, Ben?"

Ben did not always agree with what his sister said, but in this case he thought she was right. "Yes," he said. "It's much more fun being part of a ship school. And we learn all sorts of things about sailing and the sea."

3

"And other things too," Fee reminded him. "Maths and history and science. We study all of that as well as knots and swimming, and how to splice a rope, and …"

"… and how to rescue people who have fallen into the sea," added Ben.

Their parents thought that all of this was very useful.

"And it's great for making friends," Fee said.

"Good," said her mother. "Friends are really important."

Once again, Ben agreed. Friends were important, but sometimes friends could be a problem. And at the beginning of that exciting new term on the *Tobermory*, Ben realised that he had a major problem – with his best friend.

Ben's best friend on the *Tobermory*, and probably in the world, was Badger Tomkins. This was not his friend's real name, but it was the name that everybody had always used. Some people – although this was probably untrue – said that Badger had forgotten what his real name was, and that even his parents had trouble remembering it. That can sometimes happen when somebody has a nickname. When their real name is used they might look blank and say, with a puzzled look, "Who? Me? Are you talking to me?"

Badger came from New York, where his father ran a large business. Badger was not quite sure what this business was, but he knew that it involved a lot of talking on the telephone and shouting. Badger's father was always so busy with work that he had little time left for his son. He was not deliberately unkind to him, but they hardly ever did anything together.

Badger

Badger's mother also seemed to have far too much to do to give him much attention. She played a lot of tennis, and although Badger would try to watch her tennis matches, he very quickly became bored. He also felt that she was a bit too competitive. If she did not win, she would storm off the court, sometimes even throwing her racquet down on the ground. That was not the way you should play tennis, thought Badger.

"You must have a really interesting time at home," Badger once remarked to Ben sadly. "Your parents take you on their submarine, don't they? And they talk to you, I guess."

Ben did not know what to say. It can be difficult to say very much when you know that a friend is unhappy. You feel that you should say something like "Cheer up" or "Things can hardly be that bad." But sometimes your friend can't cheer up, no matter how hard they try, and sometimes things actually are every bit as bad as they seem to be.

Ben and Badger shared a cabin on the *Tobermory*. They were on Middle Deck, on the port, or left, side of the ship. In this cabin were two hammocks – the swinging beds in which sailors have always slept – two lockers for clothes and other personal possessions, and a small table with a shared chair. There was also a porthole that had to be kept closed most of the time but that could be opened in good weather.

Sharing a room with somebody else can be difficult. It often happens that people who have started off sharing as friends after a few days feel desperate to get away from each other. This may be because one person is tidy, while the other is not. It may be because one person is very quiet when asleep, while the other mumbles or coughs or snores loudly. Or there may be many other reasons why sharing simply doesn't work. It had never been like that with Ben and Badger. They liked sharing a cabin, and they enjoyed talking to each other at night after lights out. Often they would lie there in the darkness and talk for what seemed like hours before sleep covered them with its soft blanket of silence. And then, in the morning, they would find that they still had things to say, and would carry on talking until they tumbled out of bed to begin the day.

But now Ben found that sharing with Badger was just not what it used to be. Something had happened to his old friend, and he could not work out exactly what it was. It was not that he looked any different – there was no mistaking him for somebody else – but when it came to the way he spoke, then he had clearly changed.

"Did you have a good holiday?" Ben asked Badger when he came into the cabin at the beginning of the new term and started to unpack his bag.

"Yes," came the reply. That was all, just: "Yes."

Ben asked his friend whether he had gone home. "Yes," came the reply.

"To New York?" asked Ben.

"Yes."

Ben frowned. Surely Badger could say something more than yes. New York was an exciting city, and there was always a lot going on there.

"I wish I could go to New York," said Ben. "What do you think I should do there – if I ever go?"

At first this question was greeted with silence. Then, rather grudgingly, as if he did not really want to answer, Badger said with a shrug, "I don't know. I'm sure you could find something to do."

Ben stared at Badger. This was not like the friend he had known for so long and with whom he had shared so many adventures – the friend who was usually more than happy to talk about all the things he had been doing. He wondered whether he should ask him if there was something wrong, but decided not to say anything just yet. There are times when people do not feel like talking, and it is best to leave them alone. Usually they snap out of their mood sooner or later, and return to normal. That would probably happen to Badger, Ben thought.

Ben busied himself with his own unpacking. He hoped that Badger would start to talk, but he did not. Badger simply slumped on his hammock and buried his nose in a book. Ben's friend might not want to talk, but there were plenty of other people who did, and Ben now set off to find them. "I'm going up on deck to see if everyone else is back," he said.

There was a grunt from Badger – just that, a grunt, and nothing more. Ben hesitated at the door, glancing quickly at his friend. If Badger was going to be rude, then he would at least let him know what he thought about his behaviour. So rather than say anything, Ben slammed the door behind him as he left the cabin. That would let Badger know how he felt, and that, perhaps, might bring him to his senses.

Up on deck, Ben found his sister standing near the foremast, talking to Poppy Taggart, one of her closest friends on board the *Tobermory*, and the girl with whom she shared a cabin. They were looking at some photographs that Poppy was holding. Poppy came from Australia, and was usually unable to go home for the holidays because the journey took far too long. This time, however, she had been able to spend a whole month with her family, helping to shear the sheep on their farm. Like Ben and Fee, Poppy lived on Middle Deck – one of the three decks on

Poppy

which students on board the *Tobermory* had their cabins. In fact, Poppy was the Senior Prefect of Middle Deck, which was an important position.

Poppy greeted Ben with a smile and showed him the photographs. There were some of her parents' farm and some of her whole family around a campfire in the bush. In one of the pictures, Poppy was crouched beside the fire, blowing on it to get it going. Hanging just above the embers was a large tin can, blackened by smoke.

"That's a billy can," Poppy explained. "That's me getting the billy going to make tea." In the background behind her was a large pool, surrounded by eucalyptus trees. "That's a billabong," she added.

The photographs reminded Ben of the voyage that the *Tobermory* had made to Australia recently. That had been a real adventure and it had made him keen to get back there as soon as he could.

Poppy asked about Badger. "Is he coming on deck? I think I saw him walking up the gangway earlier."

"He's here," said Ben. "But …"

When he did not finish, Poppy sensed there was something wrong. She looked at him expectantly, waiting for him to say more.

"Well?" Poppy prompted.

"He didn't say much," Ben told her. "I asked him about the holidays and … well, he just said yes or grunted."

"That's odd," said Poppy.

She remembered that Badger's parents were usually too busy to take much notice of him. Perhaps that was the reason why he had come back so unhappy. "Did you ask him if there was anything wrong?"

Ben shook his head. "He didn't want to talk," he said.

Their conversation was cut short by the arrival of Angela Singh and Tanya Herring. They were close friends and had spent the school holidays together.

Tanya had been a stowaway on the *Tobermory* after running away from her cruel aunt and uncle. They were meant to be looking after her but they had done no such thing, forcing her to work long hours in their dog kennels. Tanya's father, a sea captain, had been missing at sea for years, and although he was thought still to be alive, nobody knew where he was. Tanya was sure that had he known about her treatment at the hands of her aunt and uncle, he would have come to rescue her. But he did not know, and so she was left with nothing but a vague hope that one day she would meet him again. Eventually, she had decided to run away, and had ended up hiding on the *Tobermory* until she was discovered. When Captain Macbeth heard her story, he decided that Tanya could have a free place on board and be given the same chance as every other member of the school. That had made Tanya happier than she had ever been before.

Angela had been particularly kind to Tanya and had invited her to spend the holidays with her family. They had all gone camping in France for a few weeks, and she and Angela now showed the others photographs of their trip. They had met a family who lived in a limestone cave beside a river, and had been shown round this unusual home with its walls of stone and its floor of compacted earth.

Tanya Herring

"It's really comfortable," said Angela. "It's warm in

Angela Singh

winter and cool in summer. And you don't have to worry about any holes in your roof."

Ben listened and looked at the photographs, but he was still thinking about Badger. He was worried, and began to wonder if there was anything he had done to offend his friend. If Badger was still so unfriendly tomorrow, he would tackle him about it. He would say that he was sorry if he had done something wrong, and that he would never have done anything to offend him deliberately. If that did not work, then … he did not know what to do.

The thought of spending a whole term sharing a cabin with somebody who would not talk to him was not a happy one. In fact, Ben could not bear the thought of that and decided that if things did not improve he would have to ask to be moved. Captain Macbeth would occasionally allow people to change cabins, although there had to be a good reason for it. Ben wondered what the Captain would say if he went to him and explained that his best friend was no longer talking to him? Would that count as a good enough reason to change cabin?

There was a lot to do on board that first day back. Decks have to be scrubbed every single day, whether a ship is at sea or in port, and this kept Ben busy that afternoon. His friend Thomas Seagrape was with him in the group assigned to this duty, and they chatted as they emptied the buckets of seawater they had used to make the boards of the deck spotless. There was no sign of Badger, but Ben had not expected to see him, as they were on different work rotas and Badger was probably on sail-room duty. That was harder work, which involved the unfolding of spare sails that had been stacked away while the ship was in port.

Ben thought that Badger might be in their cabin when he returned from deck duty, but there was no sign of him. The other boy's possessions had all been stacked away, and there was a spare pair of deck shoes placed neatly beside his hammock, but apart from that there was nothing to show that anybody else shared the cabin with Ben.

There was no time to think about this, though, as Captain Macbeth was due to address the whole ship's company up on deck, and everybody had to be there to hear what he had to say. This happened at the start of every term, and it was at this meeting that he would say where the *Tobermory* would be sailing to. That was always an exciting moment, as this would be the first that anybody heard of where they would be spending the next few weeks, or even the next few months.

Ben made his way up to the main deck, thinking about what the Captain might say. Fee and Poppy were already up there, and he was not surprised to find them discussing where the ship might be going.

"Somebody told me it was Greece," said Poppy. "I hope they're right."

Fee looked dubious. "I heard it was Iceland."

Amanda Birtwhistle said she saw Mr Rigger carrying a book about Iceland under his arm. "Why would he be reading about Iceland if we weren't going there?" she asked.

Ben shivered. "I hope it isn't Iceland," he said. "Iceland sounds a bit cold."

Poppy disagreed. "It may sound cold," she said, "but remember: this is summer."

"And they have all those hot springs," Fee pointed out. "And those jets of water that shoot up into the sky. What do you call them – geysers? And volcanoes."

"We'll see," said Ben. "We won't have long to wait. Captain Macbeth will tell us soon enough."

He looked around the deck, hoping to see Badger, but there was no sign of him, and he wondered whether he was still down in the sail-room. But then he spotted him, and what he saw made him catch his breath.

William Edward Hardtack

On the other side of the deck, in a small group all by themselves, were the three people Ben liked the least. Ben usually got on with most people, and he was not one to hold a grudge against anybody else. But these three were hard to like, no matter how much you tried. They were known as Hardtack and Co., after their leader, William Edward Hardtack. The other members, always at Hardtack's side, or lurking somewhere behind him, were Geoffrey Shark, with his characteristic shark's-fin hairstyle, and Maximilian Flubber, with his prominent ears that waggled every time he told a lie – which was quite often.

Like others, Ben had tried to see some good in these three. Most people, he felt, were a mixture of good and bad, and he thought that if people gave Hardtack and his friends the chance to be

Geoffrey Shark

Maximilian Flubber

pleasant, they might rise to the challenge. Unfortunately, any friendly word to them would be met with a scowl or, what was worse, a sarcastic remark. So if someone asked Hardtack, in a perfectly friendly way, how he was, they would be greeted with, "What's that got to do with you?" or "How I'm feeling is none of your business." Or sometimes they would get no more than silence.

It was not just rudeness that this trio was famous for: they were selfish and lazy, and tried, if at all possible, to get out of doing their share of the tasks that everybody on board had to do. If he was on deck-scrubbing duty, for instance, Shark would only pretend to scrub the boards, carefully avoiding the hard work needed to get the grime off the wood. And when none of the staff were around, he would simply lean on his brush and chat with his friends, resuming work only if one of the officers came on deck and could see what was going on.

In the mess hall, Hardtack and his friends were well known for their greed. Every time cake was served after the main course at lunch, Flubber would elbow other people out of the way to cut three very large pieces for himself, Shark and Hardtack . There was never enough left for everyone else. As you can imagine, nobody liked that.

In spite of this, Ben thought that if there was one member of Hardtack's gang who might be persuaded to behave a bit better, it was Flubber. There had been an incident in the past, when the *Tobermory* had been sailing around the Australian coast, when Flubber had shown a better side of his nature. Ben felt that if only this could be encouraged, there was some hope for him. The problem, though, was Hardtack's influence. William Edward Hardtack, it seemed to Ben, was the sun around which Geoffrey Shark and Maximilian Flubber revolved as minor planets. *Sometimes it must be hard*, he thought, *to overcome the gravity of a bigger star.*

And now, as he looked across the crowded deck, he saw that Badger was standing with the infamous three. And what's more, he was talking to Shark and smiling.

That was what had made Ben draw in his breath. Badger – his best friend – had said no more than a few words to him this term, yet here he was chatting away quite happily to Geoffrey Shark, of all people.

Poppy noticed the direction of Ben's gaze. She, too, drew in her breath when she saw Badger.

"Do you see what I see?" Ben whispered to Fee.

Fee nodded. She looked at her brother, who was

There was no sign of Badger in the cabin.

Badger was talking to Shark and smiling.

Geoffrey Shark would only pretend to scrub the boards.

Flubber's view of fairness ...

Shark's

Hardtack's

Flubber's

now staring down at the deck, misery written all across his face. There are few things worse than being abandoned by somebody you thought of as your friend. She felt for Ben, and wished she could say something to make him feel better. But she could not think of a thing

Captain Macbeth

that she could say, and so Fee had to stand by and watch as Ben shot a glance over towards Badger and then immediately looked away.

Captain Macbeth came on deck, together with other senior members of staff. There was Mr Rigger, the First Officer, whose famous moustache acted as a weather vane in windy weather so you could tell which direction the wind was blowing in; Miss Worsfold, who taught geography and had once been an excellent kite-surfer; and Matron, who in addition to supervising the wellbeing of everyone on board was also an expert high diver.

Mr Rigger

Matron

Everyone stopped talking as the Captain stood before them and cleared his throat. "Good evening, everybody," he said. "I have an important announcement to make about where we'll be going this term."

The whole school was quiet, hanging on the Captain's words.

"Greece!" whispered Poppy.

"Not Iceland!" Ben said, under his breath.

"Scotland," announced Captain Macbeth.

Ben's new cabin-mate

"Scotland?" muttered Poppy. "But we're already in Scotland."

She was not the only one to be surprised. Nor was she the only one to be disappointed – there had been some who were hoping for New Zealand or the South Seas, and they looked at one another in dismay.

"So we're not going far at all," Thomas said to Ben. "We may as well stay right where we are – in Tobermory harbour."

But Captain Macbeth had more to say. "Now, I know that some of you may be a bit disappointed," he said. "And I can understand why. I know that it's nice and warm down in the South Seas …"

"And there are coconuts," Poppy said under her breath. "There are no coconuts in Scotland."

"But," Captain Macbeth continued, "we shall still have lots of interesting sailing. We're going, you see, to St Kilda."

Poppy looked quizzically at Fee. "Saint what?" she asked.

Fee was about to explain when Captain Macbeth continued. "St Kilda is a small group of islands about forty miles west of the Outer Hebrides. You may think that's not far – and I suppose it isn't – not when you think of how wide the Atlantic Ocean is. But it's not at all easy to go there as the seas can be rough, and you can only land if the wind is in the right direction."

Ben was pleased. He liked the Scottish islands, and was as happy going there as he would be visiting Greece. What is more, they had learned a bit about St Kilda the previous term from Miss Worsfold. She had told them all about the history of the small cluster of islands that make up the St Kilda group.

Miss Worsfold

People had lived there for a long time, Miss Worsfold explained. Their lives had been hard in such a remote place, and eventually things became too difficult and they had had to leave. It was a sad day for them when they said goodbye to the island that had been their home for many hundreds of years.

Having given them the information about their destination, Captain Macbeth went on to deal with various other subjects. There was a new teacher to be introduced, Mr Stevenson, who would share the teaching of maths and navigation with Mr Rigger. Then Matron stepped forward and told people about the importance of wearing clean socks and brushing their teeth properly after each meal. Mr Rigger came after Matron – he had something to say about safety on deck, especially when climbing up the *Tobermory*'s high masts, which the young students often had to do in order to tend the sails. Then, when Mr Rigger had finished, the assembly was dismissed.

Ben glanced across at Badger. His friend was still standing next to Shark, and when Hardtack moved off, followed by Shark and Flubber, to Ben's utter dismay he saw Badger go with them.

Nothing could have been clearer – Badger had joined up with Hardtack and his gang. The sight made Ben feel sick. How could Badger, his best friend and cabin-mate, team up with people like that? But that seemed to be what had happened. If the evidence of Ben's own eyes was anything to go by, Badger had crossed over. He had joined the enemy.

Ben decided to have it out with Badger. His father had always told him that if there is something bothering you, it is better to say what it is, even if that means ruffling feathers. Ben liked that expression – "ruffling feathers" – because it made him think of what it would be like to stroke a bird the wrong way. It would make the bird – and whoever was stroking it – feel rather uncomfortable.

It might ruffle Badger's feathers if he asked him why he was spending so much time with Hardtack, Shark and Flubber, but that would just be too bad. If a friend does something stupid or out of character, then they can't be surprised if others are puzzled by their behaviour. That was the case here, thought Ben. And if Badger's behaviour had to be explained, the only person who could do that was Badger himself.

Ben could not do it over dinner. Although Badger was eating at the same table, he sat at the far end, next to a couple of boys whom neither of them knew very well. That hurt Ben. The thought that Badger was now avoiding him altogether rubbed salt into the wound. It was bad enough that Badger had little to say to him, but it was all made far worse by the fact that he now seemed happier to sit with people who weren't even his friends.

The moment to confront him came later, at the end of the day. This was the time when everybody was in their cabin, just before lights out. Even if Badger had wanted to avoid Ben, it would be impossible to do so then.

Ben felt his heart beating loudly as he prepared

himself to challenge his friend. At last, after Badger had laid down on his hammock and was studiously reading a book, completely ignoring him, Ben plucked up the courage to speak.

"All right, Badge," he said, using the shortened form of Badger's name that he often used.

Badger looked up from his book. His expression was cold. "Please don't call me that," he said.

Ben's face fell. "But I've always called you Badge," he protested. "Always …"

Ben did not have time to finish what he was going to say.

"My name's Badger," interrupted Badger coldly. "I don't call you something different from your real name, do I? So please call me by my proper name in future."

Ben struggled to regain his composure. "All right, Badger," he said at last. "I want to ask you something."

Again Badger cut him short. "I'm busy," he snapped. "Can't you see? I'm reading."

Ben drew in his breath. "Yes, I can see that," he said. "But that doesn't stop me from speaking to you. I can't help it if you're going to be so rude and read when I'm trying to speak to you."

Badger's response to this was to carry on reading. It was as if Ben were simply not there.

"What's wrong with you?" Ben demanded. "Ever

since we came back, you've ignored me. I tried to ask you what you'd done in the holidays, and you wouldn't tell me. I tried to be friendly, and you just cut me dead. And then …"

Badger lowered his book. "I wish you'd shut up," he spat out.

For a moment Ben did not know what to say. He and Badger might have had their odd differences of opinion in the past – as all friends do – but they had never spoken to one another like that. Badger had never told him to shut up before, and Ben would never have said such a thing to Badger.

At last Ben recovered. "You can't tell people to shut up if you don't like what they're saying," he blurted out. "You can't ignore things by just telling people to shut up."

Badger sighed. "You know what, Ben?" he said. "You really bore me."

He had only uttered a few words, but each one cut like a knife. And Ben, hurt more than he could say by Badger's words, did shut up.

They prepared for bed in silence, and when it was time to switch out the lights, Badger did so without even asking Ben if he was ready. Ben, in fact, was not ready, and had to make the last few preparations for bed in near darkness. He looked across the cabin to where Badger lay on his hammock. There was a little moonlight coming in through the porthole and he could just make out the shape of the other boy – the dark shape of one who had suddenly stopped being a friend and who, for reasons Ben thought he might never understand, had now become more than a stranger.

Every day, immediately after breakfast, Captain Macbeth set aside time for any student of the *Tobermory* to come to his cabin and speak about anything that was troubling him or her. It did not matter how junior they were – everyone had that right from their very first day on board. On a school ship, this is particularly important, as it means that if somebody is bullying somebody else or behaving badly towards them, the victim can always go right to the top to report it.

So, with a heavy heart, Ben decided to make his way to the Captain's cabin the next morning. He did so reluctantly, as he knew how busy Captain Macbeth would be just before the ship was due to leave port. And when he got to there, his fears about disturbing him were confirmed. Just as he was about to knock on the door, he heard Mr Rigger's voice inside, and realised that the two most senior officers were discussing some important mechanical problem that had arisen in the engine room.

But Ben knocked anyway and was immediately answered.

"Come in," shouted Captain Macbeth.

Ben entered the Captain's cabin. The Captain and Mr Rigger were not alone. In the middle of the floor sat the Captain's dog, Henry, a well-known and popular member of the *Tobermory*'s crew. Ben liked Henry, and Henry liked him, and the dog showed his pleasure at seeing Ben by wagging his tail vigorously and then jumping up to greet him. On the other side of the cabin, the Captain was poring over some papers that Mr Rigger was showing him. Mr Rigger turned round and frowned, obviously irritated by the disturbance.

Captain Macbeth glanced at Ben. "Hello," he said. "Just wait a moment, MacTavish." Then he turned to Mr Rigger and said something about talking about the engine-room problem a little later on. Mr Rigger nodded and made his way out of the cabin.

Ben stood in front of the Captain's desk, feeling very uncomfortable.

"All right," said Captain Macbeth. "What is it, MacTavish?"

"I'm sorry to bother you, sir," Ben began.

The Captain smiled. "Don't you worry about that," he said. "That's what I'm here for." He paused, and then went on, "So how can I help?"

Ben had rehearsed what he wanted to say, and continued. "I was wondering, sir, if I could change cabins. I don't like to be difficult, sir, but I'd be much happier in another cabin. Same deck, of course, but a different cabin – sharing with somebody else."

Captain Macbeth frowned. Reaching for a list he kept on his desk, he consulted it briefly and then looked back up at Ben. "Ah yes, of course, you share with Badger Tomkins."

Ben nodded.

The Captain raised an eyebrow. "It's odd that you should come in here asking for a move."

Ben swallowed. "I don't want to make a fuss, Captain."

But making a fuss was not what Captain Macbeth was referring to. Now came the bombshell. "It's odd, because your cabin-mate has already been in. Badger came to see me last night, after dinner, to ask if he could change cabins. He wants to share with ..." The Captain paused as he looked at his list once more, but Ben had a strong feeling he knew what he was going to say.

"He wants to share with Geoffrey Shark," said the Captain. "He wants to move to Upper Deck."

Although Ben had anticipated what was coming, actually hearing it still came as a shock. Shark!

The Captain fixed Ben with an enquiring look. "Have you two boys fallen out over something?" he asked.

Ben was not sure how to answer. "I don't know, sir," he began. "I didn't start it, if you know what I mean. I didn't pick a fight with him."

The Captain sighed. "We all have to get on with each other, you know," he said. "That's one of the most important rules on a ship. We have to get on with each other, because when we're at sea we have to live and work together twenty-four hours a day. You can't have disagreements with people."

Ben said that he understood that well. "I promise you, Captain, it's nothing I've done. Badger stopped talking to me – just like that. And when I tried to speak to him he was unfriendly and angry. I'm not making this up."

The Captain's stare was long and penetrating. "You know what, MacTavish?" he said at last. "I think I know what you mean. There's something odd about him wanting to share with Shark. Those two boys don't seem to have much in common, do they?"

"No, they don't, sir."

"Nonetheless, I gave him permission," said the Captain. "There's no point in keeping two people together if they're going to end up at each other's throats. But that means I'll have to put somebody else in with you."

He looked at his list. "There's a new boy, from Ireland, who'll need a bit of help to settle in. Are you prepared to look after him? Show him the ropes?"

Ben nodded. "I'll do my best, sir."

"In that case, I'll put Rory Quinn in with you,"

said the Captain, making a note on his list. "And listen, if I may give you a bit of advice, MacTavish – sometimes things go wrong with a friendship. Friends can do strange things on occasion. But my advice is: never give up on a friend. Give them the chance to come back to you, and never, ever, close the door. Keep the door open for a friend to come back."

He looked at Ben and waited for him to show that he understood what had been said. Ben nodded. He had understood.

"That will be all," said the Captain. "I'll get Mr Rigger to send Quinn down to you."

Ben left the Captain's cabin. He knew that what the Captain had said about never giving up on a friend was true, but he was not at all sure that the old Badger would ever come back. He thought: *I've lost the best friend I've ever had*, and the thought stayed with him all the way back to his cabin. And when he opened the door, he saw that Badger had already moved his things out.

CHAPTER 3

Rory to the rescue

They set sail that afternoon. The morning had passed quickly, with all hands helping to load provisions, making sure that everything was stowed away safely in lockers, and tackling all the last-minute tasks that must be done before a ship leaves port. Everybody had something to do. Ben was in the team that was responsible for unpacking food, stacking away countless tins and bags of flour, making sure that boxes of eggs were tucked away safely in lockers so that the movement of the ship would not break them, and packing butter and other perishable things in the ship's great walk-in fridges.

Cook supervised all that. He rushed around, barking orders and making sure it all went according to plan. No one argued with Cook, and no one tried to sneak a taste of anything without his permission – unless they were very foolish, or greedy. A boy called Wallace Springleg, well known for his sweet tooth, was once spotted by Cook just as he dipped a finger

Cook

into a large jar of jam – meaning only to taste it, of course, but it was a bad mistake on Wallace's part.

"Springleg!" roared Cook. "Was that your finger I saw in the jam?"

Springleg, caught unawares, froze. "I was just …" he began.

Cook was not prepared to listen to any excuses. "No jam for you, my lad!" he shouted. "No jam this term."

Tanya had been standing nearby. "Oh, Cook!" she pleaded. "Wallace can't help himself when it comes to jam. He really can't. Please don't be too hard on him."

Cook glared at the greedy boy. "All right," he said. "You'll be let off lightly this time, but this is your last chance – your very last chance."

Wallace Springleg looked relieved. "Oh, thank you, Cook," he said. "I promise I won't do it again."

"I should hope not," said Cook. "Dirty fingers stuck into the food are unhygienic." He paused. "One hour of onion duty for you, young man."

This was Springleg's punishment, and it was not

a pleasant one. Onion duty, which involved peeling a large pile of onions, was probably the least popular of all kitchen tasks. People who did it cried and cried because, as everyone knows, peeling onions always makes your eyes water.

Fee and Poppy were on laundry duty. A ship full of people needs a large supply of towels, and these have to be folded and put in cabins. Once they had done this, there were various other tasks that Matron had for them, including handing out soap, shampoo and tubes of toothpaste. This kept them busy until lunch-time, which was just a quick snack, as there was no time to waste if the *Tobermory* was to leave on the outgoing tide.

At last everything was ready. The signal flag announcing the ship's departure – the Blue Peter – was run up, and then, with a great creaking and clanking, the anchor chain was pulled in. The anchor itself came up covered in mud, and it was the responsibility of Angela, Tanya and Amanda Birtwhistle to wash the mud off with a high-pressure hose. Once this was done, the last few links of chain could be drawn in and the anchor stowed safely under the ship's prow.

Ben stood at the ship's rail and watched the town of Tobermory with its pretty coloured houses slip away behind them. Large white seagulls dipped and wheeled behind them, screeching to one another.

They were used to following fishing boats and would be hoping for scraps of fish to be thrown out. After a while, realising they would get nothing from the *Tobermory*, they went off in search of better pickings.

They headed first north and then west, passing the great headland of Ardnamurchan. It was a clear day, with good visibility, and from where he was standing on deck, Ben could make out a cluster of islands off their starboard side. There was Skye, one of the biggest of the Scottish islands, with its towering mountains, soft blue in the distance. There was the island of Rum, a great sugarloaf rising out of the smooth surface of the sea. There was the tiny island of Muck, with its low hills and concealed harbour. And there, far away on the horizon, was a thin strip of land that was the Outer Hebrides. They would have to sail round those islands to reach St Kilda, far out in the ocean to the west.

The wind was in their favour – a stiff south-westerly breeze that quickly filled each sail as it was unfurled. With the ship's engines turned off, the wind was powerful enough to propel the ship at ten knots across the blue expanse of sea.

They could not do the whole of the journey that day, and would sail first to a small island called Canna, where they would anchor for the night. Then, the following morning, after breakfast, they would continue to the Outer Hebrides. That journey would take them across the Minch, a stretch of water known for being rough if a big wind blew up.

Thomas Seagrape

They arrived at Canna shortly before six. Because it was summer, darkness only came much later, and the sun was still blazing brightly in the west. Once the anchor was down and safely embedded on the floor of the bay, Mr Rigger announced that a liberty boat – one of the *Tobermory*'s small rowing boats – would take people ashore if they wanted to explore the island before dinner.

Ben found himself going ashore with Rory Quinn, his new cabin-mate, and his friend Thomas Seagrape. Thomas had come to the *Tobermory* all the way from the Caribbean, where his mother was the skipper of a small ship that sailed between Jamaica and some of the neighbouring islands.

Now, in the company of Thomas and Rory, Ben set off to take a look around the small island. They climbed a hillside, startling grazing sheep that obviously saw few visitors, and then made their way down to a small cove. There was a tiny beach there – just big enough to allow a rowing boat to land – and on it they discovered a washed-up piece of wood that looked as if it had once been part of a sailing ship.

"Do you think this comes from a shipwreck?" asked Rory.

Ben examined the piece of wood. It was curved, like the ribs of an old wooden vessel, and there were rough, uneven holes where nails had once been. It must be very old, he thought, as the action of the sea had made the edges smooth.

He answered Rory's question. "Probably. There have been plenty of wrecks around here."

Thomas added something that he had heard from one of Mr Rigger's history lessons. Mr Rigger taught naval history as well as seamanship, and his lessons in the history of sailing were one of the most popular classes on the ship. "Mr Rigger told us," Thomas began, "that there were wreckers around here. Over a hundred years ago."

Ben shivered. He had read about wreckers, people who lured ships to their doom by making fires on cliffs. Thinking the fire was there to guide them, and confused in the darkness, sailors would steer their craft onto rocks. As the tide went out, the wreckers would comb the shore for the washed-up cargo from the shipwreck. They would also carry off what was left of the ship itself, stripping its broken timbers and anything else of value that they could salvage. It was hard to believe that people would do such a terrible thing – but they did.

Rory looked at his watch. "We need to get back," he said. "The boat will be leaving in half an hour and Mr Rigger said we mustn't be late."

They left the piece of timber on the shore where they had found it. Following the rough track that led back up the hill, they made their way towards to the bay. This took them across a wide field bordered on all four sides by a wall made of uneven stones, stacked one on top of another. They noticed a group of grazing cattle not far away – the small, Highland cattle that peer out from under shaggy fringes of their caramel-coloured coats.

Having no time to waste, the three boys took no notice of the cattle and hurried across the field. But that did not stop the cattle from noticing them. As the boys came closer, one of the cows, who had a calf with her, lowered her head and looked angrily in their direction. Then, without warning, she began to run towards them, bellowing aggressively. This breed of cattle is famous for fiercely protecting its calves, and this cow was now proving just how much that reputation is deserved.

It took the boys a few moments to react, but once they realised what was happening, they all took flight together.

"Run for it!" shouted Ben. "As quick as you can!"

They knew that safety lay over the wall. They did not have far to go, and could all easily have made it, had it not been for Ben's failure to see a twisted tree-root in his way. Catching his shoe, the exposed root brought him to the ground with a thump, and he landed flat on his face, the wind knocked out of him and a sharp pain stabbing his leg. Glancing back from behind the wall, Rory, who had made it to safety with Thomas, saw Ben on the ground and the furious cow gaining on him.

From where he was, all Ben saw was the grass in front of him. Then, moving his head slightly, he saw the cow rushing forwards, head lowered, ready to stamp on him. But then he suddenly saw something else. Rory had jumped back over the wall and was running towards him, waving his arms and shouting at the top of his voice. It took Ben a moment or two, but then he realised what Rory was doing.

Completely unconcerned for his own safety, Rory was doing his best to distract the angry cow. And it worked. Hearing the shouts of the other boy, the cow suddenly stopped in its tracks, bellowed a warning, and then changed direction. It was a dangerous thing to do, but it gave Ben the time he needed to get to his feet. His leg felt sore but, with difficulty, he was able to run. Reaching the safety of the wall, he hoisted himself up and over it, just in time to see

Rory doing the same thing – only a few paces ahead of his pursuer.

They were both safe. Had the cow reached either of them, it could have been a very different outcome. Cattle are heavy, and have sharp horns.

Ben looked at his two friends. "We made it," he said, his voice flooding with relief. And then, turning to Rory, he said, "You saved my life. Thank you!"

The other boy seemed embarrassed. "I didn't really," he protested. "And anyway, you'd have done the same for me."

Ben thought that was not the point. It did not matter whether or not he would have done the same thing for Rory – the important thing was that Rory had acted with astonishing bravery. And it was not as if Rory was an old friend, somebody he had known for years – the two of them had only just met. An old friend might be expected to take risks for you, but would you expect the same of somebody you barely knew?

Rory looked at his watch. "It's getting late," he said.

Ben nodded. "Yes, we should get back. But let me say this, Rory: I really owe you one."

"Nonsense," said Rory dismissively. "Nobody owes anybody anything."

Thomas gave the new boy a friendly pat on the back. He had seen clearly what had happened, and he would not forget it in a hurry. Rory was a good friend to have, he decided, and he thought that Ben was lucky to share a cabin with him.

Fortunately for Ben, he was not badly hurt. When he got back to the *Tobermory*, he made his way, hobbling a bit, to the sick bay, where Matron examined his leg and pronounced it unbroken.

"You've twisted your ankle," she said. "But don't worry, it'll heal quickly. I'll rub some of my ointment on it, if you like."

"Thank you," said Ben.

Matron's ointment was famous. It had a strong smell and warmed the skin. Matron used it for just about everything, and it always made people feel much better. The recipe was a secret known only to her and Cook, who prepared it for her in the galley of the *Tobermory*.

"Mind you," said Matron, as she worked the ointment into Ben's ankle, "it could have turned out much worse, couldn't it?"

Ben nodded. "The cow would have been on top of me if it hadn't been for Rory Quinn. I think he saved my life."

"Rory Quinn?" enquired Matron. "Is he that new boy from Ireland?"

"Yes, this is his first time on board," said Ben. "We're sharing a cabin."

Matron frowned. "You and Rory? But I thought you shared with Badger Tomkins."

Ben took a moment to answer, as losing the friendship of Badger still hurt, and it was not the sort of pain that could be helped by Matron's ointment. "Badger and I used to share," he replied, "but he's moved out."

"Oh yes?" said Matron, curious to know why the two boys were no longer sharing, but it was clear that Ben didn't want to say any more.

"And are you and Rory getting on all right?" she asked.

Ben nodded. "I think we'll be fine," she said.

"Well, he's certainly very brave," Matron said. "It sounds like he's a good friend to have."

Ben agreed. "Yes, I think he is."

Applying a little more ointment to his ankle, Matron gave it a final rub and told him he was free to go. He should be careful about doing too much running about over the next day or two, but he would be fine. Ben thanked her.

That evening, as they prepared for bed, Ben was keen to know more about Rory and asked where he had been at school before joining the *Tobermory*.

"Ireland," said Rory. "Have you ever been to Ireland, Ben?"

Ben told him that he hadn't. He was thinking,

though, of Rory's answer. It did not tell him all that much, he decided, and so he asked, "Where about in Ireland?"

Rory Quinn

"Dublin," said Rory, and then immediately changed the subject and began to quiz Ben about the Outer Hebrides.

Rory was keen to know more about their voyage, and Ben told him what he knew about the islands they would sail past the following day. He and Fee had been there several times with their parents in the family submarine. They had visited a stone circle where, thousands of years ago, there had been a human settlement, and he spoke about that for a while. Then Rory asked Ben about the staff. Did he like Mr Rigger? Was it true that Matron was an expert diver? What about the Captain's dog – was it really true, as he had overheard somebody say, that Henry had once rescued a mermaid?

Ben answered as best he could. When it was time for lights out, he realised that although he and Rory had been talking for a long time, he had found out very little about the other boy. All he knew was that he was Irish, that he had gone to school in Dublin, and a few other minor details. He had discovered that Rory had once had a dog. He had learned that Rory had a brother who was younger than he was and who was keen on football. But that was about it.

Ben was puzzled about this. He knew that you don't have to tell your friends everything about yourself. He knew that there are plenty of people who do not like to say much about where they come from, about what they like, or about who their friends are, but it was unusual to be quite so secretive. He wondered whether Rory was hiding something from him. And if he was, then what could it be?

Once he asked himself that, he started to think about various possibilities – many of them ridiculous. Everybody knows that if you are running away from something, one of the options is to go to sea. People have always done that. Had Rory done something – perhaps even committed a crime – that had made him run off to join the crew of the *Tobermory*? Or what if he had run away from home and found some relative who had been prepared to pay for him to go off to ship school? That was just possible, Ben decided, although unlikely. If there were a mystery surrounding Rory, Ben suspected it would be something different. But it could still be a surprise, and Ben hoped that sooner, rather than later, he would find out what it was.

Badger turns violent

"This is a very famous stretch of water," said Miss Worsfold to her class the next day. "Look out of the portholes, everybody, and tell me what you see."

Fee, who was sitting next to Poppy in Miss Worsfold's geography class, exchanged glances with her friend. Miss Worsfold was well known for asking trick questions. A simple question would seem to have a simple answer, but this might be quite different from the answer that the teacher expected. And when Miss Worsfold finally gave the answer, it always seemed so obvious.

Amanda Birtwhistle, who was sitting next to one of the portholes, craned her neck to look out, and then turned back to face the class. "Sea," she said. "There's sea outside, Miss Worsfold."

A couple of the boys, including Wallace Springleg, laughed at this response. "That's what you usually see when you look out of a porthole," said Wallace. "You see sea." And then he added, "See?"

Amanda Birtwhistle

There was laughter – and a smile from Miss Worsfold. "That's true," she said. "There's certainly sea out there. But what else?"

Amanda peered out of the porthole once again. "An island in the distance," she said. "A big one. That must be …"

"Skye," said Miss Worsfold. "Remember, we sailed past the Isle of Skye yesterday. And if you look the other way you'll see – in the distance – some more islands: the Outer Hebrides."

There was a long pause.

"But some parts of the sea are more interesting than others," Miss Worsfold said at last. "Some parts of the sea have a bit of history connected with them. And this part, everybody, has some very special history."

It was at this point that Fee remembered. She had read about this stretch of sea, and now it came back to her. She put up her hand.

"Yes, Fee?" said Miss Worsfold.

"It was a long time ago," Fee began. "There was somebody called Bonnie Prince Charlie who claimed to be King of Scotland, and the whole of Britain too. He was in France, I think, and …"

Now Poppy remembered too. "Yes, of course. He was in France but he wanted to come back to claim his throne from the people who had taken it. And he was chased through the Highlands and eventually had to flee."

Miss Worsfold nodded. "Exactly. And he had to get over to Skye – a very difficult crossing in a small boat, and dangerous too. He was disguised as a woman. He wore a dress so that he would not be recognised."

She paused. "This is the precise route he took. If we could go back a few hundred years we might see his boat crossing right here."

Everybody was quiet for a moment as they imagined what it would be like to make the journey all the way across to Skye in a tiny little rowing boat.

Miss Worsfold now went on to remind them about St Kilda, the group of islands the *Tobermory* would visit once they had sailed round the Outer Hebrides. Life had been particularly hard there, she said, because the islands were so isolated.

"Forty miles may not sound like very much today," she said. "But in those days boats were much slower and very few people made long sea journeys. Or, if they did, they didn't make them without a very good reason."

"How did they live?" asked Wallace Springleg. "What did the people on St Kilda eat?"

Poppy smiled, and nudged Fee. "Wallace is always thinking of his stomach," she said.

Miss Worsfold gave the answer. "Birds' eggs," she said. "Birds' eggs and fish. And sometimes a bit of mutton." She paused. "Oh, and seaweed for their greens. They would also dry the seaweed and make flour out of it. They used the flour for bread."

Wallace wrinkled his nose. "Disgusting," he said. "Birds' eggs? Disgusting!"

"If you had nothing else," said Miss Worsfold, "then you had no choice."

"You'd eat birds' eggs if you were hungry enough, Wallace," whispered Amanda. "You'd eat anything."

"What happened to the people?" asked Poppy. "Are they still there?"

Miss Worsfold shook her head. "No," she said. "You can still see their houses, but nobody lives there permanently now."

"Did they have to leave?" asked Fee.

"They agreed to go," said Miss Worsfold. "They decided that there were too few of them to survive right out in the Atlantic. That was almost ninety years ago. They loaded all their possessions onto boats and brought them over to the mainland. They took all their animals too, except for some sheep, which were too wild to be caught, so they left them behind."

For a few moments, nobody spoke. It seemed so

sad, thought Poppy, to leave the place you lived and say goodbye to it forever. She wondered what it would be like to visit the houses the islanders had abandoned. Would they be exactly the same as they were on the day that everybody left? Were they about to visit a ghost island?

"I'll show you some pictures," said Miss Worsfold.

For the next half hour, she projected them onto the classroom screen, and everybody sat in silence and stared at images of a lost and almost forgotten world. Some of them showed people of their own age, standing outside their schoolroom in bare feet. The sun was shining on their faces and they were smiling.

It seemed to Poppy that they wanted to say something – perhaps about what it was like to live on a remote island, cut off from the rest of the world and only visited every few weeks by a boat that brought supplies from the mainland. She looked at the faces more closely. Did they know, when those photographs were taken, what was in store for them? That is the strange thing about old photographs. Often we know what lay ahead for the people we see in pictures, while they themselves had no idea. We know their future, but they didn't.

Later that day Ben and Fee both had a long maths lesson with Mr Rigger. Rory was in the same group, as were Badger and Amanda Birtwhistle. Amanda was very good with figures, and could do complicated sums in her head almost as fast as most people could do with a calculator.

"It's not all that hard," she would say. "I don't really have to think about it. The answers just come into my head."

"You're really lucky," said Fee wistfully. Maths was not her best subject, though she tried her best.

Ben was a bit better at figures than his sister, although he had never been quite as good as Badger. If Amanda got top marks in every maths test, then Badger was usually in second place.

They sat in the classroom, trying hard not to be distracted by the sea outside. Ben would far rather have been out on deck, feeling the wind in his hair, than listening to Mr Rigger talk about mathematical problems. And there was another reason why he would have preferred to be up on deck, and that was because it was painful for him to have to sit in the same class as Badger and be ignored by him.

As they had filed into the classroom at the beginning of the lesson, Ben, who had decided that despite their row he would behave in a perfectly friendly way, had said good morning to Badger, but had simply been given a nod of the head in return. Not a word did his so-called friend speak to him; not a simple hello, or even an enquiry about how Ben was. Nothing. Just silence.

That morning, Mr Rigger was getting his class to tackle some simple problems.

"Now," he said, "here's something for you to work out. Are you ready? Right, if it takes one deckhand two hours to scrub forty square metres of deck, how long will it take three deckhands to scrub a hundred and twenty square metres of deck?"

Amanda's hand went up within seconds. Fee frowned, and started to jot down various figures on a piece of paper. Once she had done that, she frowned even more, rubbing out most of what she had just scribbled down.

Mr Rigger saw that Amanda was ready to give the answer, but he decided to ask Badger instead.

"Your turn, Tomkins," he said. "You should have no difficulty in giving me the answer."

Badger had been staring down at his desk. Now he looked up. "Two days?" he said with uncertainty.

Amanda could not control herself and burst out laughing at Badger's answer. Mr Rigger frowned. "Are you trying to be funny?" he asked severely.

Badger looked miserable, and it was clear to Ben at least that he had not been joking.

Badger tried again. "Ten hours?" He paused, and then, seeing Mr Rigger's look of disbelief, he said, "I mean, eight hours."

Mr Rigger shook his head. "What's wrong with

you, Badger?" he asked. "You're normally good at this sort of thing."

Badger did not reply. He was aware that all eyes were on him, and he squirmed in embarrassment. Watching this, Ben felt sorry for him. It was clear to him that Badger had not been paying attention. He must have been thinking of something else altogether.

Ben was sitting at the next desk, and, leant over to Badger. "Two hours, Badge," he whispered. "Two hours – not eight or ten."

It was not something that Ben would normally have done. Students were not meant to help each other with the answers, and if Mr Rigger saw that, there would be trouble. But watching his old friend struggle, Ben's every instinct was to help him, and so he did.

Fortunately for Ben, Mr Rigger had turned his back for a moment and had not seen or heard what was going on. But even if Badger could then have given the right answer, he failed to do so. Instead, he turned to Ben and give him a withering look. It was the sort of look that said: *Mind your own business*. It was the sort of look that said: *Don't dare speak to me!*

Ben was not prepared for this response, and Badger's cold stare struck him like a slap in the face. "I was only trying to help," he muttered.

Mr Rigger heard that. "What was that,

MacTavish?" he snapped. "Have you got something to say to the class?"

Ben shook his head. "Sorry, Mr Rigger," he said. "I was just muttering to myself."

"Well, please don't," said Mr Rigger. Then he turned to Amanda, who had put up her hand again. "Very well, Amanda. Let's have the answer."

"Two hours," said Amanda, giving Badger a pitying look.

"That's right," said Mr Rigger. "The amount of deck is three times larger, but there are three times as many people working. So the answer is that it would take the same time as it takes one deck hand to do forty square metres. Does everyone understand?"

They all nodded, except Ben, who was staring at the floor in his misery. It had been bad enough when Badger had refused to talk to him, but the look that Badger had just given him was far more hurtful. It was a look of … Ben struggled with the thought. It was a look of hatred – there was no other word for it. Badger hated him. It was hard to utter the word, *hate*, even to himself, but what other word was there to express that look of sheer loathing? And what had he done to deserve it? He had never addressed a cross word to his friend. He had never let him down in any way at all. He had never sided with others against him. There was no reason at all why Badger should behave that way towards him. It was not only puzzling, it was deeply and painfully wounding.

"But what if one of the deck hands is lazy?" Rory Quinn suddenly asked. "What if he sits about and doesn't pull his weight?"

"Just like Flubber," muttered Fee under her breath.

In spite of himself and in spite of his hurt feelings, like everybody else Ben was amused by Fee's remark. He imagined how long it would take Flubber to scrub a hundred and twenty square metres of deck all by himself if he had to.

"It would take him forever," he whispered back to Fee.

They both smiled at the thought. But Ben's smile did not last long, as he went back to thinking about Badger's peculiar behaviour. People did not act like that for no reason, and he decided that there must be something seriously wrong for Badger to behave in a way that was quite out of character. He would have to try to find out what it was. But he had no idea how to do that, as every effort to communicate with Badger so far had been rebuffed. Did that mean, after all, that he had no alternative but to stand on the sidelines and watch as things went from bad to worse for his old friend?

Classes had been over for a while by the time the *Tobermory* reached the shores of South Uist, one of the islands of the Outer Hebrides. Approaching the bay where they were due to anchor, all hands were on deck, helping to take down the sails that had carried them so quickly and smoothly across the Minch.

Fortunately, the wind had dropped and this made the task of lowering the sails easier, but such work can still be risky business even in calm weather. This is because you have to climb up rope ladders to the yard arms, the horizontal spars of wood from which the sails are suspended. Climbing a rope ladder is not easy at the best of times, but when the ladder is swinging with the movement of the sea, it is much harder. You have to keep your head; you have to look steadily up at the rungs of the ladder above you rather than down at the sea below. If you look down, you can quickly become dizzy and lose your balance. It is dangerous work, but it has to be done.

Ben and Thomas had been sent up together by Mr Rigger to deal with a small sail that needed to be furled up and lashed securely. They did this quickly, as it was something they had both done many times before. Then they began to make their way down the rope ladder back to the deck.

Geoffrey Shark and Badger had been working on another sail further up the mast. They, too, had completed their task and were coming down on the same ladder, just a little bit above Ben and Thomas.

Thomas reached the deck first. He looked up to see that Ben was about five rungs above him, and above Ben, getting rather close, thought Thomas, was Badger.

"Careful!" Thomas shouted up to Badger. "Don't crowd him!"

But Badger either did not hear Thomas, or chose to ignore him. Suddenly, Ben felt a sharp pain in his right hand. He had been gripping the rung above his head when Badger, coming down above him, stepped on it. This made Ben lose his grip and fall.

Thomas later told Poppy and Fee exactly what happened. "I had reached the deck," he said. "I was standing there, looking up at Ben, who was just above me. Badger was above him, with Shark up at the top. I saw Badger getting too close to Ben and I shouted out to him to be careful. Now I think about it, I'm sure he ignored me and put his foot down deliberately on Ben's hand. Of course Ben had to let go of the rope – you can't keep hold of something if somebody else is standing on your hand, can you?"

Poppy and Fee could hardly believe what they were hearing. "And then?" asked Poppy.

"Then Ben fell," Thomas continued. "He wasn't all that high off the ground, but still far enough for him to hit the deck with a real thud.

"If I'd been standing a bit closer I could have tried to catch him and break his fall. But I wasn't close enough. Luckily he wasn't really hurt – he could have broken a bone if he had been just a bit higher."

"Forty miles may not sound like very much today," Miss Worsfold said. "But in those days …"

Ben and Thomas had been sent up to deal with a small sail that needed to be furled up and lashed securely.

Suddenly, Ben felt a sharp pain in in his right hand.

"And Badger?" asked Fee. "What did Badger do? Did he say he was sorry?"

They waited for Thomas's reply, but both she and Poppy knew what it would be before he spoke.

Thomas shook his head. "He laughed. And Shark thought it was funny too. He said, 'Watch how you go, Butterfingers!' Then they went off together, leaving Ben to pick himself up off the deck."

The three friends looked at one another with dismay. Up until now, Badger's bad behaviour had simply consisted of rudeness and silence, but this was far more serious.

"We have to do something," Poppy said. "We can't let this go on."

Fee and Thomas both agreed, but when Poppy went on to suggest that they should tell Captain Macbeth about it, Thomas seemed unwilling. "I said that Ben should do that," he said. "But he said he didn't want to. So I offered to go myself, and that made him anxious. He said that it would only make matters worse, and that the best way of dealing with things like this is to ignore them."

"You don't ignore bullying," said Poppy defiantly. "That's how bullies get away with it."

Fee was uncertain. "I suppose it *is* bullying, isn't it?" she asked.

"Of course it's bullying!" snapped Poppy. "Badger's not just been rude to Ben, he's even tried to hurt him."

"Why don't you talk to Ben, Fee?" suggested Thomas. "See if you can persuade him to go to the Captain."

Fee pointed out that Badger might simply claim it was an accident. "After all, we don't have any real proof," she said. "Anyway, Ben doesn't always listen to me, you know. Sometimes brothers and sisters don't agree, even if they are twins."

"All right, then," said Poppy decisively, "I'll speak to Ben and see if I can get him to do something."

Fee said she thought that was a good idea, but she was not sure how her brother would react. She knew he could be stubborn once he had decided to do – or not to do – something. But the thought that Ben could have been hurt by Badger made it impossible to sit back and do nothing. She remembered something her mother had said. *Don't leave things too late. The longer you leave them, the harder they are to put right.* Yes, she thought, that was true – that was definitely true. Perhaps she should remind Ben of that.

A mysterious journal

It was a long sail the following day. At five in the morning they left the bay where they had spent the night, and by breakfast time they were already rounding the southern tip of South Uist. To their south lay the island of Barra, and to the west was the open sea. Beyond that, thousands of miles across the Atlantic, were Greenland and Canada and the United States. St Kilda was before that, of course, less than fifty miles away, but this was open sea and the swell was large enough to be felt in every part of the ship as she ploughed through the waves.

The wind had picked up again and it was coming from just the right direction to allow them to follow a direct course to St Kilda. Captain Macbeth announced at breakfast that he expected them to make landfall in about five hours as long as the wind kept up. They would anchor, he said, in Village Bay, off the main island of Hirta – the only place that provided any shelter. Then they would go ashore in the afternoon, and there would be several hours for everybody to explore the island before returning to the *Tobermory* for dinner.

There was a high level of excitement on board. There were to be no lessons, although Mr Rigger would be holding one of his special knot-tying classes on deck for anybody who was interested. These were popular sessions, and just about everybody attended, including Henry, who loved to sit on the edge of the group, chewing on a piece of rope as if he were trying to work out how to tie a knot with his teeth.

It was Poppy who noticed that Hardtack and his friends, who now, of course, included Badger, were not at the knot-tying class.

"Where do you think they are?" she asked. "It's odd, because they all fancy themselves as champion knot-tiers."

Fee shrugged, as did Ben. "I don't care," he said flatly.

Poppy took the opportunity to ask him if he would speak to the Captain about what had happened on the rope ladder. "You can't let Badger get away with something like that," she urged. "It was really dangerous. And who knows what he might do next?"

Ben looked away.

"You have to do something, Ben," Fee implored. "Poppy's right, you know."

Ben turned around. "Just leave it," he said. "It may have been accidental after all."

Poppy and Fee exchanged glances. At least they had tried, and if Ben was not prepared to do anything, they could hardly force him. For now, Poppy decided, they would have to leave things as they were. She knew that at heart Badger was not really like Hardtack, Shark and Flubber, and she was sorry that he might end up getting into serious trouble because of his new friends. But she did not say anything, as she could see that Ben was miserable enough already.

"All right," Poppy said to Ben. "But I'm telling you, Ben, if Badger tries to bully you again, I'm going straight to Captain Macbeth. I don't care what you say. I won't stand by and let a bully get away with it."

Ben looked at her, but said nothing. At that moment, Mr Rigger started to explain a complicated new knot, and everybody's attention was focused on that. And it was while they were struggling with the new knot that they heard a cry from the lookout. It was Wallace Springleg, who was high up in the crow's nest, shouting, "Land ahoy!"

Knots were forgotten in the excitement. Even Mr Rigger joined the rush to the port railings from which, on the distant horizon, a smudge of dark blue could be seen.

"St Kilda," said Mr Rigger. "There it is."

The wind was now was even stronger and the sails needed to be adjusted in order to stop the boat from leaning too far over. This done, the *Tobermory* cut through the waves with all the determination of an athlete trying to reach the finishing line of a race. Spray and foam were thrown up by the prow, and those standing nearest the railings felt the salt water on their faces. Nobody minded, though. After all, in no time at all they would be dropping anchor and seeing, for the first time, the famous island.

Fortunately, the wind was in just the right direction to allow the great sailing ship to nose her way into the sheltered waters of Village Bay. There were just a handful of other boats bobbing at anchor – including a powerful motor boat that had brought visitors and a polished racing yacht with fine teak decks and shiny fittings. It looked out of place here, and there was no sign of life on board. Ben looked closely as they passed it and saw its name – *Swordfish* – painted in black letters on the bow. There were also a couple of rowing boats used by the island's caretakers tied to moorings near the shore.

With a great clanking, the anchor chain slipped down into the sea below. When the anchor touched the seabed, the chain went slack, allowing a good length of it to lie out across the mud and seaweed below. The weight of the chain was just as important in keeping the *Tobermory* from drifting as the heavy hook of the anchor itself.

The liberty boats were prepared and lowered into the water. In small groups the excited students made the short journey to the pier. There they clambered up over barnacle-encrusted stone to set foot on the soil of St Kilda. Above them were hundreds of puffins, those strange seabirds with their rainbow-coloured beaks. The birds nested not far away, in large colonies, on the face of steep cliffs, from which they launched themselves into the clear Atlantic sky down towards the sea in search of fish.

"This is amazing," Ben said to Poppy.

Poppy agreed. "It feels so deserted, though," she said, pointing to the line of abandoned stone cottages on the hillside in front of them.

"Shall we go and take a look?" asked Ben.

"Mr Rigger says there's a museum," said Fee. "He said it shows you what life was like when people still lived here."

"Let's explore a bit first and then go and see," said Poppy.

The museum was in one of the cottages. These had thick stone walls and low ceilings. The windows, which faced the bay below, were small, making the rooms inside dim, even in the full light of the summer afternoon. There were several guardians who lived on the island, looking after the museum and houses and showing visitors around. One of them was sitting in a chair near the door when Poppy and Fee went in with Ben and Rory.

The guardian showed them an album of photographs. The pictures, all black-and-white snaps taken with an old box camera, showed the island families leading their daily lives. There was a picture of the island school – a one-room schoolhouse with a black-board at one end of the room and a double line of desks. A small number of children – no more than twelve or fifteen – were seated at these desks, staring at the camera. Then there was a picture of a woman cooking on an open fire, stirring the pot while her children looked on.

"They didn't have much money," said the guardian. "It was a tough life. They gathered feathers from seabirds and sent them over to the mainland. They were paid for that, but it was hard work."

"And seabirds' eggs?" asked Poppy. "We heard they climbed up the cliffs for those."

The guardian nodded. "They climbed up, or were lowered from the top on ropes."

He showed them a picture of a boy of about their age dangling on the end of a rope. Far below him, churning white and angry around the rocks, was the sea.

Then the guardian got up and opened a cupboard at the back of the room. "This is something you might like to see," he said. "It was sent to us by the grandson of one of the people who left the island all those years ago. It was his grandfather's diary, and he wanted it to be looked after in the museum here. He was a fisherman."

They gathered round the guardian as he opened a well-worn old journal. The pages inside were discoloured and brittle, but the writing was still clear.

"He described the fishing trips that he made," said the guardian. "He used to go over and work on one of the fishing boats on the mainland. He would be away for months at a time before coming home to St Kilda for the winter."

He turned a page. "Here's an interesting entry," he said. "He's writing about fishing in Loch Sunart. Do you know where that is?"

They all nodded, as this sea loch was not far from the *Tobermory*'s base on the island of Mull. Ben and Fee had been there too in the family submarine many times. "What happened there?" Ben asked.

The guardian peered at the page. "He said that they sailed up the loch and then went through some narrows into another stretch of water. He said they were fishing there, in shallow water, when their nets got caught up in something on the sea-bed. He was a strong swimmer, this man, and a good diver too, so he went down to see if he could see what had snagged them."

They were listening intently. "And did he discover what it was?" asked Fee.

The guardian turned a page. "Yes," he said. "And he drew a picture of what he saw. Look, here it is."

Everyone craned their necks to get a good view. The drawing was not large, but it had been done with some skill. There was the bottom of the loch, and there was the net trailing down from above. And there was the obstruction that had snared the net.

Rory drew in his breath. "It looks like ..." he said.

"Yes," said the guardian. "It does, doesn't it? A Viking ship."

For a moment nobody said anything. Then Ben asked, "Were the Vikings in Scotland?"

The guardian seemed surprised by the question. "They certainly were," he said. "Many hundreds of years ago, of course, but they were here. They came over from Scandinavia in their longboats. People were terrified of them."

"But that one sank?" asked Rory.

"Yes," said the guardian. "I have no idea what happened, but something obviously went wrong."

Ben leaned forward to examine the drawing more carefully. "Do you think it's still there?" he asked.

The guardian shrugged. "The fisherman doesn't say exactly where he found the wreck," he said. "All he said was that it was near a place where a river flowed into the loch. And that there was a waterfall

Above them were hundreds of puffins, those strange sea-birds with their rainbow-coloured beaks.

The museum was in one of the cottages in which people used to live.

WILDLIFE PEOPLE PLACES

"It looks like ..."
"Yes," said the guardian. "A viking longboat."

further up the river, whose water was very dark because of all the peat soil around there. That's all."

The guardian hesitated. "Mind you," he said. "He did another drawing – it's on the next page. This time he drew it looking from the deck of the fishing boat. I showed it to another young lad from your crew just a few minutes ago."

Ben stared at the intricate pencil drawing that the fisherman had made. It was of a view from the water, looking towards the shore. There was an outcrop of rocks, a small hill, and a steep slope beyond that. A river entered the loch next to a little beach, where the water spread out into a tiny estuary.

"Would you mind if I made a copy of that sketch?" asked Ben. He had with him the notebook and pencil he always carried when he went ashore, and so, as the guardian showed everybody else some other items in the collection, Ben made a copy of the drawing on a page torn out from his notebook.

The guardian put the old diary away and spent the next half hour showing the group some of the old agricultural tools stored in the museum. There was a rake and a set of sheep-shears, a butter churn and the blade of a scythe which had been used to cut hay.

"We have to be careful about the time," said Poppy, glancing at her watch. "We have to be down at the pier in time for the boat."

They thanked the guardian and made their way

back to the pier. Ben was deep in thought, and as they reached the pier he asked Poppy what the Vikings might have carried in their longboats.

Poppy said she thought they would have loaded the supplies they would need. "Food and weapons. Fur blankets against the cold. All that sort of thing."

"And treasure?" asked Ben.

"Perhaps," said Poppy. "They used to go off and steal people's valuable property. Gold plates, perhaps. Silver ornaments from churches and monasteries. They stole all that kind of stuff."

Ben said nothing for a few moments. Then he said, "If there is treasure, I wonder if it's still there?"

"Where?" asked Poppy.

"On the wreck of that longboat," Ben replied.

Poppy smiled. "Do you fancy yourself as a treasure-hunter, Ben?" she asked.

Rory had overheard Ben's question. "Yes," he said. "I think Ben could be right. There might be Viking treasure there – even now."

"Maybe," said Poppy. "But maybe not. Who knows?" She grinned at the two boys. "Anyway, we're not going anywhere near there."

Rory shook his head. "That's where you're wrong, Poppy," he said. "I was talking to Mr Rigger and he told me that after we leave here, we're going back to Mull. Perhaps we could sail across to Loch Sunart and look for the wreck."

Ben looked thoughtful for a moment. "I want to look at the charts," he said.

"Ask Mr Rigger, then," said Poppy. "He'll show you."

Once back on board, Ben asked to see the nautical charts, which showed in detail the coastline, the islands and the depth of the water. Mr Rigger accompanied him to the Captain's cabin. Captain Macbeth was not in, but Mr Rigger knew where the charts were kept. He took a folder out of a drawer, and after selecting one of the maps, laid it out on the Captain's table and pointed out to Ben where they were – on the small circle of green that was St Kilda – and where they were going next.

"We'll sail back the way we've come, and past the top of Mull towards Tobermory," said Mr Rigger, tracing a line with his fingertip. "Now, where was it you thought we should go? Loch Sunart, was it? That's the mouth of Loch Sunart there. There's a good anchorage beside this little island here."

He pointed to a small island lying just off the mainland, not far beyond the entrance to the loch. Ben studied the chart carefully. The old fisherman's diary had said that the longboat was in a smaller stretch of water, off the main part of the loch. The position on the chart where Mr Rigger was now pointing – the place where he said they could anchor

– was very close to the entrance to a smaller body of water. Ben's gaze moved across the chart, taking in the details of what was marked on the adjoining shore. At first he did not notice it, but then he looked again, and what he saw made him draw in his breath sharply.

"A waterfall," he whispered.

"What was that?" asked Mr Rigger.

"I said: a waterfall." Ben pointed at the place on the chart near the place where a river joined the sea loch. Just a short distance inland was a waterfall, noted in small print.

Mr Rigger glanced at the chart. "There are plenty of those," he observed. "When we sail close to the coast there, you'll see waterfalls on the sides of all those mountains."

"I know that, Mr Rigger," said Ben. "But this one's special."

Mr Rigger raised an eyebrow. "I don't see anything special about it."

Ben explained what he had been told about the fisherman's journal. He wondered whether Mr Rigger would laugh at him – it seemed such an unlikely story – but the teacher listened carefully as Ben spoke.

When Ben finished, Mr Rigger stroked his chin pensively before saying anything. "That's a very interesting story, MacTavish," he said eventually. "You know, I've heard stories about Viking longboats in these parts. I've never seen any wrecks, though."

Ben was pleased that Mr Rigger was taking him seriously. "Do you think it might still be there?" he asked.

Mr Rigger shrugged. "It's possible." Then he frowned. "However, it would be difficult to pinpoint the exact place."

Ben reached into his pocket, and took out the copy he had made of the fisherman's sketch. "He drew this," he said. "This was the view from where they found the longboat."

Mr Rigger examined the piece of paper. "This is a precise copy?" he asked.

Ben nodded. He prided himself on his accurate drawing. "I tried to make it exactly the same," he said.

Mr Rigger was impressed. "That should make it easy enough to work out where the wreck is," he said. "There are reference points here." He pointed to the outcrop of rocks on the shore, then to the small hill and the mouth of the river.

Ben agreed. "Do you think that we could take a look on the way back to Mull?" he asked.

Mr Rigger thought for a moment. "For my part, I don't see why not. I'll have a word with Captain Macbeth and suggest that we stop off there. I won't say anything about treasure though – the fewer people who know about this the better," he said.

"It would be amazing if we found a sunken Viking longboat," said Ben eagerly. "Particularly if there was treasure on board."

Mr Rigger laughed. "Steady on, MacTavish," he advised. "Don't get carried away. Plenty of people think they know where to find treasure: Spanish galleons and so on. But very few – in fact hardly any – ever find anything."

"I know," said Ben. "But it's still worth trying, isn't it?"

Mr Rigger hesitated for a moment. Then he smiled and gave his answer. "Yes, why not? If nobody ever tried to do anything, nothing would ever get done, would it?" Always give it a try – that's what I say."

"Well, I say that too, Mr Rigger," said Ben. "And thank you!"

"But don't raise your hopes too high," said Mr Rigger. "There are plenty of things that can go wrong at sea, you know. You can never be sure of anything."

Ben told him that he also understood that. But for the moment, he was far too excited to think about warnings of any sort, and he rushed off to tell his friends that they might soon be on a real hunt for Viking treasure.

Dog overboard

They spent the night at anchor in Village Bay. At breakfast the next morning, Captain Macbeth addressed the whole school. As he stood up to speak, he looked anxious, and people wondered if they were about to hear bad news.

"I had hoped that we would be able to stay here a bit longer," he said. "Unfortunately, the weather forecast is not at all good. A front is coming from the west and we're due to have some unsettled weather. So we'll be heading back towards Mull at ten o'clock this morning."

This was disappointing news. Although they had seen a bit of Hirta, there was still a lot to explore. Now that would have to wait until the *Tobermory* had an opportunity to come back to St Kilda – and that might not be for many months, or even years.

Ben did not mind, though. As far as he was concerned, the sooner they got going, the sooner they would be able to look for the Viking longboat.

"That's great news," he whispered to Thomas.

"But what if there's a storm?" asked Thomas. "It could be a very rough crossing."

"We'll survive," said Ben. "We've sailed through storms before," he added.

Thomas made a face. "I get seasick if it's too rough." He looked down at his empty plate. "I wish I hadn't eaten such a big breakfast."

"We might make anchorage before the storm breaks," Ben reassured him. "And if the wind is in the right direction – which it might well be – then we'll get across the Minch all the quicker."

Outside, it was hard to imagine that bad weather was on the way. The sky was clear – at least it was clear of clouds, even if it was filled with swirling flocks of seabirds. The sun was on the water, touching it with gold. It was a fine day, and as the *Tobermory* nudged her way out of the bay, the whole school lined the railings to watch the islands slip past.

Soon they approached the steep rock stacks that stood towering out of the water like sentries guarding the main island from the open sea. They were almost vertical, but here and there were small patches of grass – tiny slanted areas of grazing for the sheep who had made their home in these unlikely places.

"Are those really sheep?" asked Poppy, as the *Tobermory* neared one of the stacks.

Fee peered at the little shapes on the patches of

green. It seemed so unlikely that anything could survive in such a barren, unwelcoming place, but as she stared at them, one of them moved, jumping from one patch of grass to another.

She became aware that Miss Worsfold was standing beside her. The teacher had trained her binoculars on the sheep and now offered them to Fee.

"Take a look," said Miss Worsfold.

Fee focused on the rock, and shivered. It seemed like the loneliest, most dangerous place she had ever seen, and yet those were … yes, they were sheep.

"These are the descendants of the sheep the islanders left behind when they went away all those years ago," said Miss Worsfold.

Poppy shook her head in astonishment. She was used to lonely places in the Australian outback, but this column of rock, this sharply rising vertical island, seemed to her to be the most desolate place she had ever seen.

The Captain was at the helm. Because the *Tobermory* was still moving under the power of her engines, he was able to approach the stack so that everybody could get a better view. The waves, though, were beginning to get a little bigger, and he was being careful not to get too close. Even so, everybody now had a good view of the stack, of the sheep, and also of a small colony of seals on the rocks at its base.

Everybody, that is, including Henry. The dog had

taken up his position at the railings, just like the rest of the ship's company. He gave a loud bark of excitement.

"Look at Henry," said Poppy. "He's just seen the seals."

Henry wagged his tail vigorously and uttered another bark. From across the water, looking back at their unexpected visitor, one of the seals raised its head and gave a bark in response. It was just like a dog's bark, though slightly higher, and it made Fee laugh.

"That seal's trying to say something to Henry," she said. "Listen, there it goes again."

Henry replied, barking back in excitement.

"He must think it's another dog," said Ben. "I wonder if … "

But he had no time to finish what he was saying, and shouted out in astonishment as Henry, quite without warning, suddenly slipped through the railings and dived headlong into the water.

"Dog overboard!" somebody else shouted from the railing. "Captain, Captain! Dog overboard!"

From where he was standing at the helm, Captain Macbeth saw what had happened and immediately gave the order to turn off the ship's engines.

For anybody to fall overboard is a very serious situation, and the same applies to a dog too. Not that Henry seemed to think so, as his head soon appeared above the surface of the water and he started to paddle towards the rocks to join the seals.

Mr Rigger was at Captain Macbeth's side, and he now gave the order for a lifeboat to be launched. "Lower Number One Boat!" he shouted as he ran across the deck to the closest lifeboat station.

This was not far from where Poppy and Ben were standing, and they were picked by Mr Rigger to join the rescue party – as was somebody else who had been standing nearby and unnoticed by Ben. That person was Badger.

Ben glanced at Badger as they clambered into the boat, ready to take their places at the oars. The other boy averted his eyes and concentrated on slotting an oar into the rowlock.

"I'll sit on this side," said Ben. "You take that place, Badger."

Badger said nothing in reply. It was as if Ben were not there at all.

Poppy noticed what was going on.

"Ben said something," she snapped at Badger. "Didn't you hear him? Have you got wax in your ears? Is that your problem, Badger?"

This was an emergency, and there was work to be done. This was not a time for petty feuds and arguments. Yet there was Badger, sitting there, ignoring Ben completely.

Mr Rigger lowered himself into the boat and took

up his position at the tiller so he could steer them carefully towards the rocks at the foot of the stack. He signalled to Poppy to release the line which attached them to the *Tobermory*, and with that they drifted quickly away from the side of the ship. They dipped their oars into the sea, and the little boat began to cut through the water, heading directly after Henry. The dog was a strong swimmer and was now nearing the rocks on which he had seen the seals.

The seals, of course, had been watching all the commotion, and being shy creatures had disappeared into the depths. They would surface again in a few moments, well away from the rocks on which they had been happily basking.

There was a strong swell. If you were in the water and wanted to clamber on to the rocks in such conditions, you would have to let the swell lift you up and then grab hold of something and haul yourself ashore. Henry, being lighter than a person, was easily carried by the water and deposited on a flat expanse of rock, like something washed up on the beach. As the water ebbed away, he gave himself an energetic shake, as dripping-wet dogs do, sending drops of water in every direction.

Henry was puzzled about what had happened to the seals – they had been there when he set out, but where were they now? What peculiar creatures they were, he thought – they had looked friendly enough from the deck of the *Tobermory*, but now they seemed to have disappeared under the water. How could they breathe down there?

The boat rowed by Ben and Badger and steered by Mr Rigger was now getting close to the rocks. Poppy, seated at the bow, reached out towards Henry, hoping to persuade him to jump back into the water and swim towards them. If he did that, she thought, she would be able to fish him out of the sea and they could take him back to the ship.

But it seemed that Henry had other ideas. Having just emerged from the sea, he had no desire to go back into it. The water was cold and he found the large swell very disturbing. No, it was far better to be safe on the rocks, even if he still felt rather wet and was beginning to shiver from the cold.

It was then that something unexpected happened. As Mr Rigger tried to steer the boat closer to the rock in order to give Henry a chance to jump aboard directly, a sudden wave coming from the side swung the boat round, causing Badger to slip. As he did so, he lost grip of his oar, which fell into the water. This was serious: with only one oar, the boat would be at the mercy of the swell and could quite easily be lifted up and smashed against the rocks. Badger, of course, knew this and realised that he must recover the oar.

Leaning over the side, he reached out for the oar. He almost succeeded in retrieving it, but when another wave made the boat lurch unexpectedly, he lost his balance, and before he could do anything about it, he tumbled into the sea.

Falling into the cold waters of the Atlantic is bad enough in any circumstances, but if it happens when you are not wearing a life jacket it is even worse. And, on top of that, if you hit your head on the side of a boat and are knocked unconscious, as Badger had done, then you are in serious trouble.

Ben realised the danger of the situation in an instant. He knew that if nothing was done immediately, Badger would sink, and would almost certainly drown. There was nothing else for it: he must dive into the water himself to rescue him.

Ben had been more careful than Badger and had put on a life jacket before getting into the boat. He knew that this would keep him afloat and enable him to bear the weight of the other boy as he swam, supporting Badger's unconscious body, back to safety.

Realising he had only seconds to act, Ben stood up and jumped into the heaving green water. It was cold, and the sensation made him gasp, but the life jacket did its work and kept his head above the surface. Looking around him, he saw Badger's motionless body, his arms spread out and his head half underwater. Striking out in a crawl, Ben made his way to Badger's side and grabbed him just as Badger was beginning to sink. Then, turning back, still gripping Badger firmly, he struck out towards the rowing boat, where Mr Rigger and Poppy were ready to haul the two boys on board.

Henry had witnessed all this from the rock. Seeing Ben dive into the water, he had decided that he would join him and had thrown himself back into the swell. Now, as Ben and the still-unconscious Badger were dragged up into the boat, Henry gave a bark to remind everybody not to forget about him. He, too, was fished out of the sea.

Meanwhile, Poppy had now managed to recover the oar that Badger had dropped. She fitted it into a rowlock and began, with Ben, to row back towards the *Tobermory* while Mr Rigger attended to Badger. He had swallowed a lot of seawater, and Mr Rigger was doing his best to pump it out of his chest. With a terrible splutter, Badger coughed up the water and opened his eyes.

Back at the ship, blankets were waiting to be wrapped around Ben and Badger and, of course, Henry. Matron had mugs of hot soup for both boys, and one for Poppy too.

Whilst he was very relieved that everyone – including Henry – had come back safely, Captain Macbeth was concerned that Badger had gone to the dog's rescue without putting on a life jacket. "You know the rules, Tomkins," he said sternly. "It was an emergency, I'll grant you that, but you might easily have drowned. Let that be a lesson to you."

As Badger looked down in embarrassment, the Captain turned his attention to Henry. "And you are *not* to chase seals," he said, in as stern a voice as he could manage. But it was a voice that was also filled with relief, as the Captain, like everybody else on board, was glad that Henry was safe. As he leant down to pat Henry, he gave him one of his favourite dog biscuits, and Henry wagged his tail in appreciation.

Word got round very quickly about how Ben had saved Badger's life, although people also whispered amongst themselves that Badger had yet to thank his rescuer.

"You'd think he'd be grateful," said Fee later, in a disgusted tone. "Badger would have drowned if it hadn't been for my brother. You'd think that he'd have had the decency to say thank you. But has he? He has not."

Ben did not say anything about what had happened. He had done what anyone would have done in the same circumstances. Of course he couldn't have just stood by and let Badger drown. And if Badger chose not to thank him, that did not surprise him: the old Badger he had once known had disappeared, and he did not think it likely he would ever come back.

That evening, when Ben returned to his cabin after dinner, he found that Rory was already there, and he was holding an envelope.

"This had been slipped under the door," he said. "It's addressed to you."

Ben examined the envelope closely. It was a plain white envelope, on the front of which was written BEN MacTAVISH in black ink. In the top left corner was the word PRIVATE, written in the same block capitals as Ben's name.

"Did you see anybody deliver it?" asked Ben.

Rory shook his head. "No. As I said, it was there when I came back. I didn't see anybody around."

Ben saw that Rory was beginning to smile. "Have you got a girlfriend?" he asked. "Maybe it's from a girl."

Ben shook his head. "I know lots of girls," he said. "But I don't know any who would want to write me letters."

"You never know," said Rory. And then he asked, "Aren't you going to read it?"

Ben turned away. He was aware that Rory was watching him, but he did not want to open the envelope in front of him. After all, it very clearly said that it was private, and he saw no reason why Rory should see it. If the envelope had been addressed to Rory and marked PRIVATE, then he would not have expected the other boy to show it to him.

With his back to Rory, Ben tore open the envelope. There was a single sheet of paper inside which had been folded twice. As he smoothed out the note to read it, Ben found that his hands were shaking. "Ben," the note began.

> I know how angry you will be with me. I know that I should have thanked you today when you saved me from drowning. You must think I'm a real rat not to say anything. Okay, I am. I've let you down in every way, but I want you to know that I don't want it to be like this. But it has to be. I'm so sorry. This is the way it has to be.

Beneath that was the signature: Badger. His friend.

Ben folded the note and put it in his pocket.

"Well?" asked Rory. "Who's it from?"

Ben shook his head. "It said private. You saw that."

Rory looked surprised. "So you're not going to tell me?" he asked.

"No," said Ben. "Sorry, Rory, but private means private."

Rory shrugged. "I don't care," he said.

Ben bit his lip. Rory clearly thought he had the right to know what was in the letter, but he had been secretive himself when Ben had asked him about his past. If Ben was not allowed to have secrets, then the same should apply to the Irish boy.

"What about you?" Ben said.

Rory frowned. "What do you mean?"

"You think I should show you a private letter," he said. "But you keep a lot secret, don't you? I mean, you haven't really told me much about yourself, have you?"

The effect of this was striking. Rory's mouth opened as if he was about to say something, but then it closed again. Then he looked down at the deck, avoiding Ben's gaze. And Ben, seeing the other boy shaking slightly, immediately felt sorry that he had spoken like this.

"I'm really sorry," he said. "That was unkind of me. I'm sorry, Rory."

Nothing more was said, but Ben continued to think about Rory's reaction to his question about secrets. His face had assumed a look that perhaps might best be described as a look of fear. And yet there they were on a school ship with lots of other people, including a whole lot of teachers. How could anybody possibly be afraid in such circumstances?

CHAPTER 7

The Viking wreck

The sail back towards the island of Mull kept them all busy. Classes had started again, and much of the day was spent on the subjects that everybody had to learn. Poppy and Fee were in a science class together and spent time in the new labs on Lower Deck. Ben and Thomas were kept busy with a history project they were doing together, as well as with some extra navigation lessons with Mr Rigger. And of course, when classes were over for the day, there were always plenty of routine shipboard tasks to be completed. Decks had to be scrubbed, ropes inspected and mended, and railings and fittings polished. At the end of the day, nobody had the energy left to do very much, and most of the *Tobermory*'s young crew would simply sit on deck watching the sun sink below the watery horizon until it was time to return to their cabins and go to bed.

Captain Macbeth had agreed with Mr Rigger's suggestion that they stop off at Loch Sunart on the way back. It took them two days to reach the mouth of the long inlet that runs into the mainland of Scotland not far from Mull.

"There's a little bay near a small island," he said. "It's well protected from any winds that might spring up, and it will be a good place for the *Tobermory* to spend the night."

They found the bay and dropped anchor just before dinner. It was a fine evening, and there was still warmth in the sun, which that far north would not set until after ten o'clock. Ben was excited: according to the charts he had consulted with Mr Rigger, the place where the Viking longboat had gone down all those centuries ago was not at all far away. In fact, when he looked out from where they had anchored, he could make out the entrance to the body of water where it lay – through a narrow tidal channel bounded by rocks on either side. This could not have been more than half a nautical mile away from where they were.

"Just think," Ben said to Thomas. "Just think – there's a Viking longboat on the seabed over there. And maybe there's treasure on it."

Thomas looked in the direction in which his friend was pointing. "Do you think we'll be able to find it?" he asked. There was plenty of treasure at the bottom of the sea in the Caribbean – or so people said – but he had never found any. Perhaps they would be luckier

– Ben seemed so sure that he had identified the place described in the old fisherman's diary.

Ben assured Thomas that there was a good chance of their being successful. "As long as nobody has got there before us," he said.

Thomas looked thoughtful. "Just imagine if we find something," he said. "What would we do with it?"

Ben had not thought about this before. "I suppose we hand it over," he said.

Thomas looked puzzled. "But to whom?"

Ben shrugged. "To a museum, I suppose."

Thomas was disappointed. "Can't we keep it?"

Ben shook his head. "Treasure doesn't belong to the person who finds it," he said. "I think you get a reward, but you have to hand it over."

Thomas liked the idea of a reward. He understood, though, why the treasure itself should be handed over to a museum. Treasure is part of a country's history, and that history belongs to everybody.

"When will we be able to go and look for it?" asked Thomas.

Ben was not sure, but later that evening he had the chance to ask Mr Rigger.

"First thing tomorrow," Mr Rigger replied. "I'm as keen as you are to start searching."

"First thing" meant after breakfast, and after

deciding the activities for the day. Since the *Tobermory* was spending the day at anchor, everybody was allowed to choose a special activity to do. Some people were planning to go kayaking, others were going ashore to go hillwalking or were going on a hike to the village at the far end of Loch Sunart.

Ben and Thomas, along with Rory, were going with Mr Rigger and Miss Worsfold to search for the Viking longboat. Poppy, Fee and Amanda Birtwhistle were also in the party, so Mr Rigger authorised the use of one of the larger rowing boats for the outing.

A few others noticed their preparations and were curious about what was being planned. One of them was William Edward Hardtack, who sidled up to Ben and demanded to know what was going on.

Ben answered politely, without giving anything away. "We're going out with Mr Rigger and Miss Worsfold," he said.

"I can see that," sneered Hardtack. "I'm not blind, you know."

"I didn't say you were," said Ben.

Hardtack took a step forward. He liked to stand close to people when he talked to them. This made them feel uneasy – which was exactly how he wanted them to feel – and more likely to do what he wanted them to do.

"So," said Hardtack, "where are you going with Mr

Rigger and Miss Worsfold? Off on some stupid search for something?"

Ben was silent for a moment whilst he considered Hardtack's question. He did not think that Hardtack knew about the Viking longboat. But then he remembered that the guardian at the museum on St Kilda had said that he had showed the old fisherman's diary to another boy just before Ben saw it himself. Could that boy have been Hardtack, or Shark perhaps? Ben tried to remember if he had seen what Hardtack and Co. were doing on the island, but he could not recall anything. Except … yes, he had seen them! He had seen them talking to somebody – a rather scrawny man with a shaggy beard – from one of the other boats that had been anchored off Village Bay. Realising that he must not give anything away, Ben simply smiled and answered, "Who knows?" And then he added, "Actually, it's just an outing. They're probably going to teach us something about rocks or seaweed, or something like that. There's a lot to learn about seaweed, you know."

Hardtack gave him a scathing look. "A lot to learn about seaweed," he mimicked. "I don't think you're telling me the whole truth, MacTavish. I think you're hiding something."

Ben took a deep breath. Hardtack could pester him as much as he liked; he was not going to tell him they were off to look for a Viking longboat, and he

95

doubted whether anybody else in the expedition party would either. And if nobody told him, then there was nothing that Hardtack and his friends could do to interfere with the search.

The weather that morning was perfect for rowing across Loch Sunart. There was a slight breeze from the south-west, but this did no more than ruffle the waters of the incoming tide.

"We'll take an outboard engine," Mr Rigger announced. "We can use it if the wind gets up, but in these conditions, I think we should row."

This was a popular decision. Rowing was one of the subjects the *Tobermory* students had to take an exam in, and any opportunity to practise was always welcome. Poppy and Miss Worsfold took the oars first, and rowed the group across to the other side of the loch. Then it was the turn of Ben and Rory, who took their places at the oars and began to row the boat through the narrow channel that led into the inlet beyond.

"That note you got last night," said Rory, as they pulled on the oars. "Was it anything important?"

Ben was surprised that Rory had mentioned the note again. "Why do you want to know?" he asked.

Rory leaned forward to pull on his oar, matching Ben's movement. "Because I can tell that there's been something really bugging you," he said.

They pulled on the oars again, and the boat slid forward through the water. The others were all talking amongst themselves, so Ben and Rory's conversation was not overheard.

Ben thought for a while, then decided to tell Rory more. "It was from Badger," he said.

Rory let out a long whistle. "Badger!" he exclaimed. "But you told me he wasn't talking to you."

"He isn't," said Ben.

"Then why the note?"

Ben said that he thought that some people find it easier to put things in writing rather than talking about them. "Maybe Badger's like that," he added.

"And what did he say?" asked Rory. "Did he say sorry?"

Ben nodded. "Sort of," he said.

Rory was about to ask another question when Mr Rigger called from the bow of the boat to "Ship oars!" – a command to Ben and Rory to stop rowing.

"I think we're in roughly the right place," said Mr Rigger. "If you look over there, you can see the top of that hill in line with the far edge of the beach."

The boat sat immobile in the water. It was slack tide now, which meant that there were no currents moving them in any direction. From where he sat, Ben looked over the side, down into the water below. Somewhere not far below them was a Viking long-boat – if the old fisherman's diary was to be believed.

And if the Viking longboat was there, then there could well be treasure too.

Miss Worsfold had brought her diving equipment with her, and now she was preparing for an exploratory dive. She was wearing a black diving suit, as the waters could be cold, even in summer. On her back, now being strapped into position by Mr Rigger, was a large tank of oxygen.

Everybody watched in fascination as Miss Worsfold made her final preparations. Diving is a dangerous activity, and it is important to be absolutely sure that everything is working correctly before you get into the water. Once submerged, a diver is at the mercy of the sea, and if anything goes wrong, the consequences can be fatal.

"Ready?" asked Mr Rigger.

Miss Worsfold gave a thumbs-up sign, and then, perching on the edge of the boat, she leant backwards, tumbling into the water with a loud splash. A second later she had disappeared under the surface, only a trail of tiny bubbles indicating that there was somebody there.

Mr Rigger looked at his watch. "Fifteen minutes," he said. "That's what she thinks she'll need."

The minutes passed slowly. They were some distance from the shore, but were close enough to see a couple of herons standing completely still at the water's edge, waiting for a careless fish to come within range of their long, sharp beaks.

Ten minutes passed, then eleven, then twelve. Mr Rigger looked at his watch again.

"Is she all right?" asked Poppy anxiously.

"I'm sure she is," said Mr Rigger. "Miss Worsfold is an experienced diver, you know."

"But what about the bends?" asked Thomas. "Isn't that a danger?"

Mr Rigger frowned. "The bends can be dangerous," he said. "Divers who get the bends have to get medical help pretty quickly."

Rory wasn't quite sure what the bends were, and asked Mr Rigger to explain.

"It happens when you come up to the surface too quickly," he said. "If you do that, then bubbles of gas can form in your blood and cause a lot of trouble. So you have to be careful and come up gradually."

Rory shuddered. He admired people who could dive under water, but he felt that it was not for him. *People are not designed to go under water*, he thought – *just as fish are not designed to be on dry land.*

Suddenly there was a commotion in the water beside the boat. Huge bubbles broke the surface, followed by a glistening rubber cap, a face mask, and then the rest of a diver. Miss Worsfold was up.

Ben and Thomas helped Miss Worsfold to get back into the boat while Mr Rigger stood by to take her oxygen tank and diving mask. Everyone was eager to find out what she had seen – if anything.

"Is it there?" Mr Rigger asked.

There was a moment of complete silence as they waited for Miss Worsfold to get her breath back.

"Yes," she said, her face breaking into a wide grin. "It's there. I saw it."

Ben let out a whoop of delight. He had steeled himself for disappointment, and this was wonderful news. "Are you sure, Miss Worsfold?" he asked.

"One hundred per cent sure," she replied. "It's covered in barnacles and weed, but the shape is unmistakable – it's a Viking longboat."

Mr Rigger rubbed his hands together in glee. "We'll have to organise further dives," he said. "We shall need to explore the wreck properly."

Miss Worsfold continued, "I wouldn't count on there being treasure, though."

Poppy had been listening intently; now her face fell. "But surely ..." she began.

Miss Worsfold explained. "As I said, I could make out the general shape under all the weed and barnacles," she said. "But I didn't see much else, I'm afraid."

Mr Rigger was not to be put off. "We can come back for a good look," he said. "I'll arrange for a diving team to be assembled. Matron likes diving, and Poppy, you're a good diver – you could dive too if you like."

Poppy readily agreed. They hurried back to the *Tobermory*. A second dive could be fitted in the following day, but more equipment would have to be prepared and time would be needed to make plans.

"I still think there might be treasure down there," said Ben to Poppy as they reached the *Tobermory*. "The Vikings were known for stealing gold goblets and things like that. They would have transported their loot in their boats."

"And if a boat sank, the treasure sank with it," said Poppy. "Is that what you're saying, Ben?"

Ben nodded. "Exactly."

Poppy was not so sure, but as a member of the diving team she would be among the first to find the treasure – if it were there. And even if it were not, it would still be interesting to see the wreck of a ship that had last sailed a thousand years ago. "This could be the biggest thing that's ever happened on the *Tobermory*," she said.

Ben agreed. They had enjoyed numerous adventures on their school ship, but this trip was turning out to be one of the most exciting voyages they had ever made.

At the same time, of course, the business with Badger was also making it one of the most troubling. Ben sighed. Badger's note might have been the beginning of some kind of resolution, but there had been nothing more since then.

Now, as he came aboard the *Tobermory*, he saw Badger standing at the stern with Geoffrey Shark. Without thinking, Ben waved to Badger. The other boy saw him – Ben was in no doubt about that – but then turned away as if Ben were not there.

CHAPTER 8

Kayaks at midnight

"Now listen, everyone," said Captain Macbeth later that evening.

He was addressing the school in the mess hall, just before dinner, as he always did when there was an important announcement to make.

"We've had some worrying news from the engine room," he continued. "The Ship's Engineer was inspecting the engines this afternoon and has discovered a serious fault. It's going to take a few days at least to fix it. Even though we're not far from Tobermory, we're just going to have to stay put for the moment."

Poppy and Fee looked at each another. Usually the prospect of spending several days at anchor in the same place would not have appealed to them very much, but with Viking treasure to look for, this delay was an enormous stroke of luck.

"We can't go anywhere until the engines are back in working order," Captain Macbeth continued. "So we shall just have to make the most of where we are. There are plenty of things to do on land around here." He pointed out of one of the portholes in the direction of a large mountain which plunged right down to the shore of the loch. "Those of you who would like to try climbing can go up there. Mr Stevenson will arrange climbing classes."

Ben liked the idea of that, but Fee did not. She had no head for heights.

"And there is a farm nearby where they would be very happy for a bit of help – for those of you who fancy yourselves as farmers."

Poppy liked the sound of doing that. Since her parents had a sheep farm in Australia, it would be interesting to spend some time on a Scottish farm. And Amanda Birtwhistle was keen on that as well. She had a soft spot for sheep, and she had already spotted some of them nibbling the seaweed at the shore of the loch.

Not everybody was pleased with the activities on offer. William Edward Hardtack could be heard murmuring something about it all being "a waste of time", and Geoffrey Shark had a glum expression on his face. But they were never enthusiastic about any of the Captain's plans, so their reaction came as no surprise.

"Boring!" muttered Shark, in a voice that could only just be heard.

Captain Macbeth looked up sharply.

"Did I hear somebody say the word 'boring'?" he asked, a note of anger coming into his voice. Captain Macbeth very rarely lost his temper. He was a fair man, who was always willing to see another person's point of view, but at the same time he was the captain of a ship – and the captain of a ship cannot allow open complaining and disobedience. Those things, as all sailors know, can be the beginnings of mutiny.

Nobody spoke.

"Would the person who said that please put up their hand," said the Captain sternly.

But no hand went up. Along with several others, Ben had heard Shark's remark, and looked across at the other boy to see if he would own up. But, like everyone else, Ben did not think he would.

It was now clear that Captain Macbeth was not going to let the matter go. On any ship, you simply cannot have people answering back to the captain or being rude to any of the officers. You have to obey the captain because the safety of the whole ship might depend on that.

Suddenly a hand went up, and the Captain looked out over the sea of heads to see whose it was.

It was Badger's.

Captain Macbeth was staring at Badger. "Boring, is it, Tomkins?" he snapped. "Well, you're not going to be bored tomorrow, young man," he continued.

"There are plenty of decks to be scrubbed."

"Yes, sir," said Badger meekly, his eyes firmly fixed on the floor.

Later that night, as they were lying awake in their cabin, waiting for sleep to overtake them, Ben and Rory discussed what had happened earlier in the mess hall.

"Why did Badger own up to it?" mused Ben. "It wasn't him at all."

"I know," agreed Rory. "It was Shark. I heard him too. I suppose he must have wanted to cover up for him. I don't understand why he would do that, but I can't see any other explanation."

"Unless he was ordered to do it," Ben said, the idea forming in his mind as he spoke. "Yes, maybe Hardtack ordered him to take the blame."

Rory said that he himself would never take the blame for what somebody else had done. And he would certainly never do anything that Hardtack told him to do.

"Yes, but you're not in his gang," said Ben. "If you're in a gang, you'd be frightened to disobey the leader. That's how gangs work."

"Who's frightened?" asked Rory, rather confused now and with a very worried look on his face.

"Badger, of course," replied Ben. As he said this, Ben thought it was Rory who seemed frightened.

Ben remembered that when he had asked about Rory's past the other boy had not told him much. It was as if he had been hiding something. Now Ben wondered whether he should ask Rory directly about his secret – if he had one.

"Rory …" he began.

"Yes?" came the hesitant reply from the other side of the cabin.

"Are you running away from something?"

It was a direct question – and sounded a bit more probing than Ben had intended. So he quickly added, "You don't have to tell me, if you'd prefer not to."

For a while there was silence.

Then Rory replied. "Since you ask, yes, I am."

"What is it?" Ben enquired.

The answer astonished him.

"Pirates."

Ben almost laughed. "Come on!" he exclaimed. "There aren't any pirates these days. That's all imagination. Storybook stuff – Captain Hook and all that."

Rory's voice was firm. "No, Ben, that's where you're wrong. There are still pirates in some places. In the Caribbean, for example. And I saw them. I was a witness."

Ben waited, eager to hear more.

"You see," said Rory, "I used to sail with my father. He was the skipper of a big sailing boat. He used to charter it out to people who wanted to spend a week or two at sea. During the school holidays I would act as cabin boy – making up the bunks and stuff like that.

"We were on a voyage one day," Rory continued, "and we noticed that we were being followed by another boat. There were no other vessels around – just us and the other boat. It was faster than ours and it soon overtook us."

Ben listened in fascination.

"They came on board," Rory said. "And they took all our valuables. Watches, jewellery and money. They stole everything."

"And they got away with it?" asked Ben.

Rory hesitated. "At first, but then they were caught when they were robbing another boat. They were put on trial back in Dublin, which is where they came from in the first place."

He paused. "I was the witness who identified them."

"And …?" prompted Ben.

"And they were sent to prison … all except one of them – their leader. They couldn't prove the case against him. He was let free." Rory paused again, and then he took a deep breath and said, "He swore to get even with me."

Ben was astounded. He was beginning to understand why Rory had been so reluctant to say anything when Ben had asked him about his past.

"The police said that I should be sent off somewhere safe," he said. "My parents thought that best place for me would be a ship school – and so here I am."

Ben apologised for having quizzed Rory about his past. "If I had known," he said, "I wouldn't have asked you all those questions."

Rory said he did not mind. It was important, though, he added, that nobody else should know who he was and why he was on board the Tobermory. "It's the biggest secret I have," he said.

"I promise I won't tell anybody," said Ben. "I really mean that, Rory."

"I trust you," said Rory. And then he added, "Time for sleep, Ben. Good night."

Ben said goodnight, but stayed awake for some time after Rory had dropped off. He had heard the most extraordinary tale, but he would never repeat it to anybody. He had given his word, and he would keep it.

Although Ben seldom had any trouble getting to sleep, he would often wake up if there was any unusual noise. This was never much of a problem, as he would usually drop back to sleep again within a few minutes. On board ship there are always plenty of noises at night, which means it is never entirely quiet. There are creaking sounds made by masts and ropes. There are gentle slapping sounds made by the waves as they break against the side of the ship. There are many other sounds too made by the wind and the water, but these are simply the constant accompaniment to life at sea.

That night, just before midnight, Ben was woken up by an unusually loud noise. At first he wondered whether he had dreamt it. He rubbed his eyes and turned over to get back to sleep. But then he heard it again, and this time he knew straight away what it was: it was the sound of oars splashing in water.

Ben slipped out of his hammock and made his way towards the porthole. The moon was high in the night sky, almost full, and it was bathing the sea and the surrounding hills in a pale, silver light. Not far away he could see the looming silhouette of the mountain that came right down to the shore against the lighter sky. It was the shape of a crouching lion, Ben thought. Everything was still – except for something moving in the water. As he peered out of the porthole and his eyes became accustomed to the gloom, he could make out a small boat being rowed across the loch.

He pressed his nose up against the porthole to see more clearly. His breath made the glass mist over, and he rubbed it with the sleeve of his pyjamas. Now he could see the shapes of two people in the boat. It was too dark to identify one of them. But there was no mistaking the other. In the half-tones of the moonlight, Geoffrey Shark's fin-like hairstyle was unmistakable.

What was Shark – and whoever was with him – doing rowing across the bay in the middle of the night? Just as he was mulling over the answer to this question Ben noticed something else. At the far end of the bay, anchored off a small, tree-covered island was another boat – not a rowing boat or anything like that, but the sort of boat that would have five or six cabins and would be capable of sailing long distances across the open sea. Even with the assistance of the moonlight, it was not possible to make out much detail, but Ben saw lights on board. One of them must be a torch, as it seemed to be flashing out a message. He drew in his breath. From the rowing boat came a quick succession of long and short flashes: Shark was replying.

It was obvious that something very strange was going on, and Ben thought he should wake Rory to tell him about it.

"Rory," he whispered, placing a hand on his cabin-mate's shoulder. "Wake up, Rory. Something's going on."

If Ben was a light sleeper, then Rory was the opposite. It took a good bit of shaking before Rory opened his eyes and looked up at Ben in confusion.

"What is it?" he muttered. And then, as he

struggled up through layers of sleep, he added, "Is it morning already?"

Ben told him what he had seen. Rory was now fully awake, and after slipping out of his hammock, he crossed the cabin to the porthole and looked out. "It's Shark!" he exclaimed. "I'd recognise that stupid hairstyle anywhere."

"I know," said Ben. "And he's been signalling to that boat over there."

Rory turned to Ben. "I think we should go over ourselves and see what's going on," he said.

"How?" asked Ben. "They've taken the rowing boat, and the other boats are all stacked away."

Rory thought for a few moments before he came up with a solution. "Kayaks," he announced. "There are two kayaks on deck. We could get them into the water without making any noise. They're not heavy."

The kayaks were special covered canoes that were popular with the students on board the *Tobermory*. Seated in a kayak, with a double-bladed paddle in your hands, you can cut quickly – and silently – through the water. If they kept far enough back, and their paddling was quiet enough, Ben and Rory would be able to follow Shark's boat without being seen or heard.

"Let's try it," said Ben.

They dressed hurriedly, putting on their darkest clothing so that they would not stand out in the moonlight. Then, as quietly as possible, so as not to wake anybody, they made their way along the darkened companionway and up onto the main deck. Just as Rory had remembered, the kayaks were there, lashed to the railings.

It only took them a few minutes to carry the kayaks down the gangplank to the small platform at the side of the ship used for getting into smaller boats or onto jetties. There they lowered the slender craft into the water and slid into the seats. Pushing themselves away from the platform, they paddled away from the *Tobermory* towards the other side of the bay. They could make out the shape of the larger boat, and they could see dim light from its wheelhouse and some of the portholes, but there was no sign now of Shark's rowing boat.

"He must be all the way across by now," Ben said, his voice barely a whisper. Sound travels very easily across open water, and they did not want to give anybody warning of their approach.

The kayaks travelled fast, and very soon they had crossed the bay. Ben spotted Shark's rowing boat tied up at the stern of the larger boat, bobbing up and down in the water. Rory saw it too and signalled to Ben to slow down. Then, pointing to the far side of the boat, he began to paddle in that direction.

They could now make out the lettering on the stern of the boat. Ben read it, and whispered it under his breath: *Swordfish*. It was not perhaps the friendliest of names. Many boats are called by amusing names, or names that at least have a friendly ring to them. There are plenty of *Jolly Dancer*s and *Good Companion*s and so on. *Swordfish* was a sharper sort of name, Ben thought – not unlike *Rapier* or *Javelin* – perhaps even rather sinister. Something was bothering him – one of those memories that linger in the mind, niggling, reluctant to go away. *Swordfish*? Ben tried hard to remember. He had seen a boat called *Swordfish* somewhere before … Then, suddenly, it came to him. *Swordfish* was the name of the boat that had been anchored in Village Bay at St Kilda. That was it: he *had* seen this boat before, and it was only a few days ago.

They heard voices coming from one of the open portholes, and by paddling very quietly Ben and Rory were able to get right under it without being detected.

Ben heard somebody cough. Then a voice – it was a man's voice – said, "Is this the Viking boat you mentioned over on St Kilda? Are you sure? And you think your crew mates might have found it?"

It was all that Ben could do to stop himself from gasping. He knew for certain now that Shark must have seen the picture of the wreck in the old fisherman's journal because Ben was positive that neither he nor any of his friends would have mentioned it to anybody else – other than Mr Rigger, of course, and

Miss Worsfold too. But they would never have passed on the information to Geoffrey Shark, of all people. No, Shark must have seen the journal himself.

The man who had asked the question now received his reply. Ben and Rory would have recognised Shark's voice anywhere. It was a slightly nasal voice, with a sinister tone to it – just the sort of voice a real shark would have if sharks could talk.

"I'm positive," Shark said. "Hardtack spoke to them and was suspicious when they said they were going to study seaweed, and I also heard something later on."

"What did you hear?" asked the man.

"I heard one of our officers talking to one of the teachers. They were discussing the Viking ship. They said there might be treasure on board."

There was silence for a few moments. Then, outside in the boat, Rory sneezed. If you have ever tried to stop yourself sneezing, you will know how difficult it is. In fact, if the sneeze really wants to come out, it is impossible to stop it. And so it was for Rory, and before he could do anything about it, the tickling in his nose had become an irresistible burst of a sneeze.

Ben caught his breath. He knew that it was not his friend's fault, but it was still about the worst thing that could have happened. Inside, the silence

In the half-tones of the moonlight, Geoffrey Shark's fin-like hairstyle was unmistakable.

SWORDFISH

AAAAAAACHOO!

Then the man said, "Did you hear someone sneeze?"

continued for a few moments more. Then the man said, "Did you hear somebody sneeze?"

Another voice – one they had not heard say anything yet – chimed in, "It certainly sounded like a sneeze to me."

At that moment, a head appeared at the porthole and looked out. A small bank of cloud had drifted across the sky, but just at that moment it moved past, allowing the moon to bathe the whole scene in a silver light. Ben, peering up towards the porthole, looked straight into the face of the person looking out. And that person was Badger.

For a moment both of them froze. The two boys stared directly at one another for several seconds, then Badger's head disappeared back through the porthole. "It was a dolphin," he said. "You know how they make that sound when they come up for air."

The man considered this for a moment, then said, "Anyway, it's late and you'd better get back to your ship. Thanks for the news, boys, and remember, there'll be something in this for you. If we get to the treasure first, you'll get a reward."

"Thank you," said Shark. "I can just imagine the look on old Worsfold's face when she gets down there and realises she's too late. And Rigger too. His moustache will hit his boots when he discovers he's missed out. Hah!"

Ben glanced at Rory and gave a signal to leave

before Shark and Badger started to row back to the *Tobermory*. Swiftly and silently, the kayaks headed back across the water.

The empty boat

Straight after breakfast the following morning, Ben called a meeting of his friends. They met in the life-jacket storeroom, a place that few people would have reason to go when the boat was at anchor. It is hard to keep secrets on a ship, where everyone lives so close to each other, but there are always quiet corners for a private conversation. This was one of them.

Poppy was there, as were Tanya, Amanda and Fee. Then there were Rory and Thomas, and Ben, of course, who closed the door once everybody had arrived.

"What's this all about?" asked Poppy.

Ben told them about what he and Rory had seen and heard the previous evening. They listened intently and nobody interrupted, except when Ben came to the part about Badger's head appearing through the porthole. That made Tanya gasp.

"Badger!" she exclaimed. "What's happened to him? He's completely changed. I always thought he was such a nice guy until this term."

"He was," said Fee. "Once upon a time, but not now."

"People change," Thomas observed. "I knew somebody back home who started off nice and then became a real bully. Something went wrong inside – I don't know what it was, but it was as if he had become a different person."

"That's what I feel has happened to Badger," Ben said. "He was my friend, you know, and then …"

Poppy looked at him sympathetically. "I know what you mean, Ben. He just changed, didn't he? Just like that."

Ben nodded. "Anyway," he said, "I thought we should decide what to do. That's why I called this meeting."

Poppy scratched her head. "It's hard, isn't it? But I suppose we have to go to Mr Rigger and the Captain and tell them. We have to warn them what these other people are up to."

"But then they'll ask us how we know," said Tanya. "That will mean Ben and Rory will have to say that they overheard them."

"So?" said Poppy. "That's what they have to do."

Rory saw what Tanya had been driving at. "But then we'll have to admit we took the kayaks and went out at night. That's against the rules."

"Rory's right," agreed Fee. "That's really serious.

If you leave the ship at night without permission, it's automatic suspension from all activities for ten days. It's a really, really strict rule."

They lapsed into silence for a moment. There was another difficulty, and Ben now mentioned it. "The other problem is Badger. If we tell them about Badger being there, then he'll be punished along with Shark."

"I suppose that's right," said Poppy.

"And they could be expelled," said Ben. "I wouldn't mind if any of Hardtack and Co. were sent away, but not Badger."

"But Badger's almost as bad as them these days," Poppy pointed out. "I don't see much difference between them."

Ben did not answer. He could see what Poppy meant, but he remembered the note Badger had written and how Badger had pretended not to see anything when he looked out of the porthole. That had saved not only him but Rory as well. So Badger was not *all* bad. Something had happened to him, but there was still, deep down inside, something good. There was a chance – a slender chance, perhaps, but nonetheless a chance – that the old Badger might come back.

"All right," said Poppy. "We won't go to the Captain. But what can we do?"

"We watch," suggested Rory. "We watch what

happens on the *Swordfish*, and if we see them heading for the dive site, we warn the Captain and Mr Rigger."

That seemed to everybody to be the best thing to do.

It was decided that when the *Tobermory* diving party went to explore the Viking wreck, Tanya would stay on board and watch the *Swordfish* through binoculars. If she saw anything suspicious, she would go straight to the Captain.

"It's the best we can do," said Ben. "It's not great, I know, but it's something."

The three divers in the diving party later that morning were Miss Worsfold, Matron and Poppy. They could not work unassisted, though, as there must always be people on the surface to keep watch and be ready to help in any emergency. That team was led by Mr Rigger, and included Ben, Fee and Thomas. Their job was to make sure all the equipment was loaded onto the dive boat, to navigate the boat to the right place, and then, they hoped, to lend a hand in loading the treasure.

Nobody spoke on the way to the dive site – the divers were all thinking of the dangers they might face underwater, while the others were all wondering what Viking treasure would look like. Ben thought it would almost certainly be gold – elaborate drinking vessels, perhaps, or ornaments for the bride of a Viking chieftain. There might be weapons, too – swords with jewel-encrusted hilts – as well as other priceless objects.

They did not take long to reach the spot. It was an isolated place, and the only witnesses of their expedition would most likely be seals. These inquisitive creatures can never resist the temptation to pop their heads up out of the water and watch whatever is going on.

And seals did appear shortly after they arrived at their destination. Four sets of bright eyes watched from a safe distance, curious to know what these unexpected intruders were up to. As the seals watched, the divers put on their face masks and Mr Rigger positioned the boat so as to be directly above the place where Miss Worsfold had found the Viking wreck the day before. With their oxygen tanks in position, the three divers leant back over the side of the boat and disappeared into the water with a splash.

"Good luck!" shouted Ben as he watched Poppy's head go under, but she would not have heard him. Soon the surface of the loch had returned to its calm, glassy state.

They waited anxiously. Eventually Mr Rigger looked at his watch and announced that the divers would surface within a few minutes. He was right, and soon bubbles were seen heralding the return of first one diver, then another and another. Helping them back up onto the boat, the first thing that Ben noticed was that the nets that the divers had taken down with them were empty. His heart sank. That meant there was no treasure.

Miss Worsfold confirmed Ben's fears. "Nothing," she said, shaking the water out of her hair. "Nothing at all, I'm afraid."

Ben looked at Poppy, who shrugged. "It's just a few pieces of old wood now," she said. "It's the skeleton of a Viking boat – covered with seaweed and barnacles. It's not very exciting, I'm afraid."

Everybody was disappointed, including Mr Rigger, who was silent for a few moments before blowing through his lips, producing a sort of *harrumph* sound that made his moustache droop in a discouraged way. Ben caught his eye – he knew how the officer felt. Like everybody else, he must have built up high hopes of a haul of treasure that would be reported in all the newspapers. Now all they had were a few ancient spars of wood, turned to coral by the action of the sea.

They packed up and made ready to go. As they did so, Ben noticed that another boat was negotiating its way towards them. At first it was too far away for him to make out clearly, but as it got nearer, there was no doubt.

"Look!" Ben whispered to Poppy. "That boat over

there. That's the boat Shark and Badger were on last night."

Poppy stared at the approaching boat, as did Fee and Thomas.

"We must tell Mr Rigger everything," said Poppy.

Ben agreed, and without wasting any time, he made his way to the other end of the boat, where Mr Rigger was helping Miss Worsfold to stow away the oxygen tanks. Mr Rigger did not want to be disturbed, but when Ben told him there was something very important he had to say to him, Mr Rigger gave him his full attention. Ben recounted everything that had happened the night before – except he did not mention that Badger had been with Shark on board the *Swordfish*. That could wait. He might have to tell him that eventually, but for now there was no need to get his former friend into trouble.

When Ben had finished, Mr Rigger reached for a pair of binoculars and trained them on the other boat. Then he lowered them and said to Ben, "There's not much we can do, I'm afraid. They're quite within their rights to sail freely around here – these are open waters."

He lifted his binoculars again and took another look. "They're watching us," he said after a while. "I'm looking straight at their captain, who's looking straight back at me."

Four sets of bright eyes watched from a distance ...

... a sort of *harrumph* sound that made his moustache droop ...

"They're watching us," he said.

"I'm looking straight at their captain who's looking straight back at me."

Thomas was impatient. "Surely we can do something," he said. "Can't we tell the police, Mr Rigger?"

Mr Rigger explained that the police would be as powerless as they themselves were. "The *Swordfish* isn't breaking any laws," he said. "Unless a wreck is officially listed as a special site, it's not against any law to look at it. After all, that's what we've just done – and we haven't broken any laws."

They were now ready to return to the *Tobermory*. As they made their way back into the main part of Loch Sunart, they passed close to the other boat, which was now preparing to drop anchor. Poppy spotted two divers on the deck. She reported this to Mr Rigger and Miss Worsfold, but once again they could do nothing but shrug their shoulders.

"They won't find anything anyway," said Miss Worsfold. "They can search and search, but they're in for a disappointment."

"Just as well," said Thomas. "If they found any treasure they would never give it to a museum. They'd just pocket it, wouldn't they?"

Ben agreed. He was pleased there was no treasure for the other boat to find, but he was sad that their own search had proved fruitless. He had read so much about people who stumbled across hidden treasure, and it had been his dream that one day it might happen to him.

A thought suddenly struck him. Ben turned to

Poppy. "Poppy," he said, "what would you have done if you were a Viking and your boat started to sink?"

"It would depend on where I was," said Poppy. "I'd be worried, I suppose. I don't think the Vikings had life jackets."

Ben agreed that she was probably right about that, but he pressed her further. "But what would you do if you were sinking right there where we found the boat?"

They both turned and looked back towards the spot where the Viking longboat lay. Then they looked towards the shore and the river that flowed into the loch, which was not a long distance away. And then they raised their gaze towards the hill beyond the shore, which was covered with trees and had rocky outcrops.

Poppy was thinking out loud. "If I had been a Viking," she murmured, "I would have tried to get ashore with the valuables. Then I'd look for a hiding place like a ..."

"A cave?" Ben interjected.

"Yes!" said Poppy. "A cave. I'd look for a cave where I could leave the treasure."

Ben smiled. "I think I'd do exactly the same thing," he said.

Back on board the *Tobermory*, Ben and Poppy were summoned to the Captain's cabin, where they found

Captain Macbeth with Mr Rigger and Miss Worsfold.

"Miss Worsfold has told me all about the dive," the Captain began. "I'm sorry it came up with nothing, but at least the wreck has been found and can be reported to the appropriate authorities. They may want to take steps to protect it. It is, after all, of historical interest."

"Yes," said Miss Worsfold. "There are marine archaeologists who might want to take pictures of it. You never know. Sometimes things that seem to be no more than, say, a heap of old stones can tell us a lot about the past."

The Captain agreed, but it was clear from the tone of his voice that there was something bothering him.

"Mr Rigger has also told me about last night," he said to Ben. "But I'd like you to tell me in your own words exactly what happened."

Ben glanced at Poppy. He had been worried he would be asked about this. Was this the moment when he would have to reveal that Badger had been on the other boat as well as Shark?

He swallowed hard. The Captain's eyes were on him. He felt nervous.

"Come on, MacTavish," urged the Captain. "I'd like to hear everything."

Ben swallowed again. Then, summoning up all his courage, he said, "Can I ask you one thing first, Captain?"

Captain Macbeth nodded. "You can ask me anything, MacTavish. That's what I'm here for."

"Would you be able to forget about something – just for a few days?"

The Captain frowned. "I'm not sure I understand what you're asking," he said. "Forget about something? About what?"

"I mean," Ben answered, "if what I told you would get someone into serious trouble, would you be willing not to do anything about it until … well, until a bit later?"

The Captain glanced at Mr Rigger, who looked just as puzzled.

But Miss Worsfold guessed what Ben was driving at. "I think there was somebody else there," she said to Ben. "There was somebody else with Geoffrey Shark – somebody you want to protect." She paused, and looked straight at Ben. "Is that right, Ben?" Then she added, "Your friend, Badger, perhaps?"

Ben nodded. It had all come out now. Badger's name had been mentioned.

Captain Macbeth cleared his throat. "I see. Well, I must say I'm not surprised. That boy has been led badly astray by Hardtack and his friends, and it's a great pity." He looked kindly at Ben. "He was your good friend, wasn't he?"

Again, Ben nodded.

The Captain continued, "You know, MacTavish,"

he said to Ben, "friendship at sea is a very important thing. You have to be able to count on your friends because you may need them to keep you – and the ship – safe."

"That's right," said Mr Rigger. "When I was just starting at sea, my life was saved by one of the other sea cadets. I'll never forget that. And years later, I was able to do something for him."

"And it hurts a lot when a friendship goes wrong," said Miss Worsfold.

The Captain had made up his mind. "I think I can give you the assurance you want," he said. "I won't do anything about Badger for the next few days. But eventually, I'm afraid, I'll have to have a very serious talk with that young man, and with Geoffrey Shark too, of course."

Ben felt very grateful. "Thank you, sir," he said. "I can't believe that Badger is one hundred per cent bad, you know."

"Nobody's one hundred per cent bad," said the Captain. "Most of us are a bit of a mixture, aren't we? We have a good side and a not-so-good side. We just have to hope that the good side outweighs the bad."

Now that Ben knew he could speak freely, he told the Captain exactly what had happened when he and Rory had paddled across to the *Swordfish* in their kayaks. The Captain listened carefully. "There's nothing we can do about those people," he said. "I've sent a message to the authorities about the wreck and I hope they'll send somebody out to take a look at it, but until they come, we can't stop others from diving there."

Poppy now joined in. "Ben and I were wondering about something," she said. "We thought that if there was no treasure on the Viking boat, then it might be somewhere else. We thought it might have been hidden in a cave nearby."

The Captain looked interested. "And you'd like to take a look for it?" he asked.

"Yes," said Poppy. "We could go tomorrow. We probably won't find anything, but at least we'll have tried."

The Captain thought for a moment, then looked at Miss Worsfold. "Would you be willing to go with them, Miss Worsfold?" he asked. "Perhaps you and Matron could both go along?"

Miss Worsfold was keen to do this.

"Good," said the Captain. "That's settled, then."

As they made their way back down the passage, Poppy looked at Ben. "What next?" she said.

"We get our team together for tomorrow," said Ben. "Fee, Thomas and Tanya, if she wants to come."

"And Henry?" asked Poppy. "It could be useful to have a dog on a treasure hunt."

Ben laughed. "Yes, I suppose he'd be good at digging," he said.

Poppy agreed. Then she looked at Ben. "You still seem a bit worried."

"Yes," he admitted. "I've got something really difficult to do, and I'm not going to put it off any longer."

CHAPTER 10

A confession

That evening there was hobby hour after dinner. This was a popular activity on board the *Tobermory* as it gave the young crew the opportunity to spend time on the different things they liked to do. Some people were in a band that practised in the mess hall, others liked to watch a movie, and others just liked to sit around and talk. It was left up to them to do as they pleased, and the members of the staff never interfered.

Ben and Thomas were planning to work on a model pirate ship they had been building. It was a complicated affair, made to scale and with intricate sails and rigging connected to the main balsa-wood hull. It was slow work, but they were pleased with the results so far and planned to enter it in a national modelling competition.

Thomas could tell that Ben was unsettled. "Are you sure you want to work on the ship tonight?" he asked after they had laid out their modelling equipment in the *Tobermory*'s workshop.

"Yes," said Ben rather absently, before adding, "Well, no, actually." And then, as an afterthought, "But I'll try."

They settled down to work, but after a few minutes, Ben stood up. "I'm going up on deck," he said to Thomas. "You carry on. I'll come back later."

Thomas shrugged. Ben was clearly in a bit of a mood, and in his experience when people are in a mood it is best simply to allow them to get over it in their own way. So he got on with what he was doing while Ben left and began to make his way up to the deck.

There were only a few people outside, even though it was a warm night and still quite light. Ben noticed Amanda Birtwhistle talking to Tanya up at the prow of the boat. They often giggled a lot when they chatted, and he could hear them now. He never found out what the joke was, though, as they always clammed up if he asked them what was so funny.

But it was not the two girls he was looking for – he was hoping to find somebody else. And now he saw him: Badger, all by himself, leaning on the stern railing, looking down at the water.

Ben approached the other boy quietly. He had become used to Badger's odd behaviour over recent days and he knew that if he called out to him, Badger might simply turn and walk away.

Badger did not see him come over, and now Ben was standing right behind him.

"Hello, Badge," Ben said.

Badger spun round, clearly taken aback by Ben's silent approach. He opened his mouth to say something, but then closed it. And then Ben noticed something he had not expected: Badger was crying.

For a few moments, neither boy said anything. In his embarrassment, Badger reached up to wipe the tears from his eyes, but this only seemed to make matters worse. Now his body was wracked by sobs, and he turned away, hugging his arms to his sides, a picture of misery.

Ben stepped forward. "Oh, Badge," he said. "You mustn't cry."

You mustn't cry is what people often say to somebody they find crying, but it is not easy advice to follow. Sometimes you have to cry. Sometimes you can't help yourself, and crying is the only thing to do.

Ben reached out. He put an arm on Badger's shoulder. He half expected the other boy to push him away, but he did not. So Ben put his other arm around his friend in an attempt to comfort him.

"Do you want to talk to me about it?" murmured Ben. "It's best to talk, you know. It really is."

At first there was no reply from Badger, but then, between sobs, he finally heard the words he had been longing to hear.

"I'm sorry," said Badger. "I'm so, so sorry."

"You don't have to say sorry," Ben said. "You really don't."

Badger's sobs were easing off now. "I do, you know," he said. "I need to say sorry to everybody."

Ben waited. If there was something that Badger needed to say, then it would be best, he thought, to give him the time to say it. And over the next few minutes that is exactly what happened.

"I have to tell you something," said Badger.

"Only if you want to," said Ben.

"I do. I have to tell you that although I hang out with Hardtack and the others, I don't really like them."

Badger looked at Ben, meeting his gaze, and Ben knew that he was telling the truth.

"I can understand that," said Ben. "But why do you do it, Badge?"

Badger hesitated. Then he confessed. "They're forcing me to," he said.

Ben frowned. Why was Badger letting them do this? Surely it would have been simple for him to go to the Captain and report what was happening? That was the policy on the *Tobermory* to deal with such behaviour. The Captain would not tolerate bullying, and bullies were dealt with firmly.

But what Badger had to say next was much more complicated than that. Ben listened in complete silence, appalled at what Badger was telling him, but saying nothing to stop the flow of the story.

"It started quite a while ago," Badger began. "Hardtack and Shark came up to me at the end of last term, when we were all about to leave the ship for home. Shark did the talking. He said that they knew something about me and they would tell the Captain about it unless I did what they said."

Ben drew in his breath. "They threatened you?" he asked.

"Yes," said Badger. "It was a threat all right."

"But what were they talking about? What did they say they'd tell the Captain?"

Badger looked down at the deck. He was clearly ashamed. "I did something terrible, Ben."

Ben drew in his breath. A part of him did not want to hear any more. Sometimes it is easier not to know certain things about our friends.

But Badger looked up now and began to explain. "Do you remember what happened last term? Do you remember how we lost one of the rowing boats?"

Ben nodded. He remembered the incident very clearly – everybody on board did, because losing a rowing boat is a serious matter.

"Well," Badger continued, "you'll remember that the boat was tied up at the side of the ship one night but was not there the next morning."

"Yes," said Ben. "I remember that." And everyone

said that it can't have been properly tied up."

"That's right," said Badger. "And they thought that the tide had carried it off."

"And it was never found," Ben added.

"No, it was never found." Badger hesitated. "Well, I was the one who tied that knot – the knot that failed. I was careless, and when the tide started to run it took the boat with it."

Ben said nothing. He had not expected this, and it was taking some time for it to sink in.

Badger continued. "Captain Macbeth asked whoever had tied up the boat to own up. I should have done that, but I was too scared. I thought I'd get into real trouble for having been so irresponsible. I just knew what my dad would say if he was asked to pay to replace it."

Ben could imagine how Badger felt. "I'd probably have felt the same," he said quietly.

"I don't think so," said Badger. "I'm a coward, you see, Ben."

Ben shook his head vigorously. "No you aren't, Badge. You're not a coward. It's only natural to feel scared of getting into trouble."

"Well, whatever it is, it was the wrong thing to do," Badger went on. "It was the wrong thing to do because by the time Hardtack and Shark came along and said they had seen me tying the knot, it was too late for me to go to the Captain. I would only have got into far worse trouble for not owning up when I should have."

"So you decided to join up with them rather than be reported to the Captain?"

"Yes," said Badger. "I did. And once I had done that, life became terrible. They like to order me about and be part of all their horrible schemes. To show how much they could control me, they told me I had to break off my friendship with you, and even hurt you."

So that explained Badger's behaviour on the rope ladder when he had trodden on his hand, Ben thought to himself.

Badger sighed, and for a moment Ben thought he would burst into tears once again. "There's no escape, Ben. I'm trapped."

Ben felt a sudden surge of anger. This anger, though, was not directed against Badger, but against Hardtack and Shark, and even against the unfortunate Flubber, who was well known as being the weakest of the trio.

There *is* something you can do, Badge," he blurted out. "You can go to Captain Macbeth right now and tell him the truth. It's never too late to tell the truth – never."

Badger did not seem convinced, but Ben could see that he was thinking about it. All that was required, he felt, was a push – just a little push to ensure that his friend escaped from the terrible mess he had got himself into.

"I mean it, Badge," he pressed. "If you go and confess everything, that will mean Hardtack and his bunch will have nothing on you. You'll be free."

"But I'll get into trouble," said Badger.

"You're in trouble already," argued Ben. "And if you don't get away from that crowd, you'll be in even deeper trouble, sure as anything."

Badger thought about it. Then, after a few minutes of silence, he said, "Will you come with me, Ben? I can't do it on my own."

Ben did not hesitate. "Of course, I will," he said.

"Come in!" called Captain Macbeth.

As they stood outside the door of the Great Cabin, Badger looked nervously at Ben. "I'm not sure …" he began.

Ben gripped his arm and gave it a squeeze. "Don't change your mind," he said. "Not now."

"But …"

Ben gave Badger's arm another squeeze. "Come on, Badge," he urged. "You're not a coward."

"Come in!" Captain Macbeth called again, slightly impatiently now.

Badger took a deep breath and opened the door. Once inside, the two boys saw the Captain seated at his desk. Mr Rigger, who was holding a chart, was standing beside him. They both looked as if they were in the middle of some complicated navigational planning.

"Yes?" asked the Captain abruptly. "Is this important? Mr Rigger and I are extremely busy, I'm afraid."

Badger lowered his eyes. "It's very important, Captain."

"Well then," said Captain Macbeth. "What is it, Tomkins?"

Badger's voice was unsteady. "I've come to tell you that I've done something stupid."

The Captain raised an eyebrow. "Something stupid? What precisely have you done?"

"I didn't tell you that I was the one who caused that rowing boat to be lost last term. I didn't pay attention when I was tying the knot. I was careless."

The Captain tensed. "Go on," he said quietly.

Badger swallowed hard and began to tell the full story. When he had finished, both the Captain and Mr Rigger were silent. Ben closed his eyes and wondered whether he had done the right thing in persuading Badger to speak up. If Badger were expelled and sent home for good, it would be his fault.

The Captain broke the silence. "Why didn't you tell me at the time?" he asked.

Badger looked miserable. "Because I'm a coward,"

he said. "I didn't have the courage."

The Captain looked at Mr Rigger, and Mr Rigger looked at the Captain.

"You're not a coward," Captain Macbeth said suddenly. "If you were a coward, you wouldn't be standing in front of me right now."

Ben felt a surge of relief. He had hoped that the Captain would be understanding. "Any of us can make a mistake," he continued. He turned to Mr Rigger. "Isn't that true, Mr Rigger?"

"Of course it is," agreed Mr Rigger. "There's nobody – not one single person – who hasn't done something stupid at some time or other."

"That's right," said the Captain. "I can't pretend I'm not annoyed with you for not coming to me earlier, but the important thing is that you've come, and better late than never is what I always say."

"Yes," said Mr Rigger. "That's true."

"I can't say that I approve of Hardtack and his friends," said the Captain. "He and Shark at least will certainly be punished for this."

Badger winced. "Do you have to, sir?"

The Captain, Mr Rigger and Ben looked surprised.

"I'd prefer it if you didn't punish them. I'd just like to tell them myself that I've had enough of them and won't take any more of their bullying. I'll feel better if I walk away from them like that."

Ben thought this was a good idea. "If you let Badger do this, Captain," he said, "then it will show them that they can't go round threatening people whenever they like. They'll learn that people can stand up to them."

The Captain mulled this over. Then he said, "Well, on this occasion I agree – if you're sure this is what you want."

Badger nodded and it was all settled. Ben, though, had a request to make. "Do you think that now this is over, Badger and I could share a cabin again?"

The Captain thought about this for a moment. "What about Quinn?" he asked. "Will he mind?"

Rory was a popular boy and had made many friends during the short time he had been aboard the *Tobermory*, so Ben thought he would be perfectly happy to have another cabin-mate. In fact, Rory had mentioned that he got on very well with another new recruit, James, who had already asked if Rory would like to share with him.

"In that case," said the Captain, "I see no problem with this."

As they left the Captain's cabin, Badger turned to Ben and said, "Thank you, Ben. Thank you for everything."

"You don't have to thank me," said Ben. "I'm your friend. You don't have to thank your friends."

But Badger knew he had much to be thankful for.

As they walked away from the Captain's cabin, both boys were happier than they had been for a very long time. They were friends again, and that counted for so much – more than he could ever say, thought Ben. And Badger thought exactly the same thing.

Treasure hunt

At breakfast the following morning Badger had to endure the hostile stares of Hardtack and Co. They had been surprised to see him sitting at his old table once more rather than with them. Ben noticed them huddled in conference before Hardtack sent Shark over to have a word with Badger.

"Hey, Badger," said Shark coldly. "Aren't you sitting in the wrong place?"

Badger looked up from his plate of scrambled eggs. "Wrong place, Geoff? No, this is where I belong, I think. Sorry. No offence."

Shark stood quite still. "Here?" he said after a while. "You think you belong here?"

"Yes," said Badger calmly. "Among my friends, you see."

Poppy had been following this exchange without saying anything. Now she piped up. "You heard what he said, Shark. What's the problem? People can sit wherever they like."

Shark looked at her scornfully. "That's what you think," he hissed. Then, turning to address Badger again, he said, "Hardtack told me to tell you that you're to come back to our table. Now."

This was too much for Poppy. "William Edward Hardtack," she said, giving equal emphasis to each part of the name. "Who does he think he is?"

Shark turned his head slowly. As he did so, his shark's-fin hair moved through the air as menacingly as a real fin cuts through water. "You'll find out soon enough, Puppy."

This was typical of Hardtack's group, who always found it amusing to change people's names. So Mr Rigger became Mr Pigger, Badger had been called The Striped One, and now Poppy was being addressed as Puppy.

"Her name's Poppy," said Badger firmly. "If you ever washed your ears, Shark, you might hear properly and get it right for once."

Ben, Fee and Poppy laughed. Shark, of course, did not think it funny. He spun round to address Badger once more. "This is your last chance, Badger," he blurted out. "You know what will happen if you don't do what Hardtack says."

For a few moments there was silence. Then Badger rose to his feet so that he was standing level with Shark. It was clear to everybody now that he was extremely angry.

"Listen to me, Shark," Badger began slowly. "Why don't you just get lost and go back to your bully boss Hardtack?"

Ben, Fee and Poppy were so thrilled to see somebody standing up to Shark that they found themselves clutching at the table edge in their excitement.

Shark leaned forward, thrusting his face almost up to Badger's nose. "You watch it, Stripe-Face!" he hissed. "If you want to get thrown off the ship by the Captain, you're going about it the right way. And what will your Daddy say when his precious little boy comes home to New York having been kicked out of school? He'll be pleased, won't he?"

Badger laughed. It was just the right reaction to make somebody like Shark feel even angrier. Nobody with a hairstyle like Shark's, thought Ben, likes to be laughed at.

"I'm warning you!" Shark's voice rose in pitch. "You know what'll happen."

Badger caught Ben's eye, and smiled. Then he turned back to face Shark. "Actually, Shark," he said calmly, "I've already spoken to the Captain about the rowing boat. I told him it was my fault it was lost."

Shark frowned. It was clear that he had not been expecting this. "You're making that up," he said.

"If you need proof," Badger said, "then ask Ben. He went with me."

"That's right," said Ben. "I did. Badger told Captain

Macbeth exactly what happened and the Captain has told him it's all right. He said that anybody can make a mistake."

Just for an instant Shark might not have believed Ben – because people often do not believe what they do not want to hear. But there was something so firm in the way Ben spoke that Shark was convinced that what Ben said was absolutely true. For a moment he hesitated, and then he turned on his heel and stomped back to his friends.

Badger sat down. He was shaking.

"Well done!" said Poppy, patting Badger on the back.

"Yes," said Ben. "Well done, Badge."

"It's great to see somebody standing up to a bully," Fee said.

Poppy agreed. "Did you see his hair?" she asked. "I think it almost collapsed with shock."

They all laughed again, and when Ben glanced across the room to Hardtack's table, he thought that Shark's famous shark's fin did indeed look a little smaller, and a bit more lop-sided, than usual.

After they had finished breakfast, there was no time to think any more about what had happened in the mess hall. The expedition to search for the treasure needed preparation, and everybody had a task or two to do before they set off. Matron had spoken to Cook about food, and he had left out supplies for picnic-lunches. Bread had to be buttered, eggs hard-boiled and a large chocolate cake wrapped in greaseproof paper. This kept Poppy and Ben busy for some time.

Fee, Thomas and Tanya were responsible for getting the boat ready, under the watchful eye of Miss Worsfold, who would accompany them with Matron and Henry, of course. Not only did the outboard engine have to be carried from its storage place, but it needed to be fuelled and clamped into position. Oars had to be found, as these would be necessary if anything went wrong with the motor. Then there were life jackets to be stacked in the boat along with coils of rope, a spade, and all the other things that a shore expedition required.

Finally, everybody had to get themselves ready. They needed to find their swimming gear, a towel and spare clothing in case they got wet. Ben wanted to take his torch too, as he thought that if they found any caves they might be very dark inside. Fee was keen to take her sketch book. She liked sketching shells, and was hoping to find some interesting examples, before realising that a treasure hunt is an exciting business and she probably wouldn't have time for sketching.

As for Miss Worsfold, she was bringing the one thing that, more than anything else, would be useful on a treasure-hunting expedition. This was a metal detector – one of those instruments that registers whether there are any metal objects buried in the ground. If there was Viking treasure near the river, with any luck the metal detector would emit a high-pitched beeping sound when it passed over it.

At last, everything was in order, and Miss Worsfold was able to give the command "Boat away!" The small vessel was lowered into the sea, and they all climbed in. With Miss Worsfold in charge of the outboard engine, they slowly chugged away from the *Tobermory* and began to make their way across the expanse of water that separated them from the entrance to the inlet. Henry barked in excitement as they drew away from the ship. Much as he enjoyed being on board, he always loved going ashore, where there were so many more smells to interest a dog.

With the tide in their favour, it did not take them long to reach their destination. After beaching the boat, they all helped pull it up over the sand. This was a lesson that Miss Worsfold was at pains to underline. "Always remember to pull a boat well up from the water's edge," she said. "An incoming tide can easily take it back out to sea when it turns."

Badger laughed. "Yes," he said. "I remember once on Nantucket I left my boat in what I thought was a safe place and when I came back it had gone. The tide had gone out and taken it."

He paused before continuing. "I suppose that

makes two boats I've lost when I think about it, though at least I eventually got my own boat back. As for the other one – well, I'm really sorry about that."

Ben was pleased to hear Badger talk like this. It showed his old friend was back again – the person who was always happy to tell a story, even if it made him look a bit foolish. It was one of the things he liked about Badger. He was not vain, and didn't take himself too seriously. He was the opposite of Shark, who had such a high opinion of himself.

And yet, Ben told himself when he thought more about it, everybody – even Shark – must have some good points somewhere. Nobody was entirely bad. Shark probably had parents who loved him and perhaps even imagined he was a popular member of the *Tobermory* crew. Perhaps Mrs Shark spoke proudly of her son and his achievements, as most mothers do. And perhaps Shark was different things to different people … That possibility made Ben think.

Miss Worsfold interrupted his thoughts. She had been listening to Badger's story, and said, "Everybody, and I mean *everybody*, has done something stupid at sea. It goes with being a sailor, I suppose."

Matron looked thoughtful. "And not just at sea," she said. "I've made a few mistakes myself, I can tell you."

Intrigued, Miss Worsfold wanted to know more. "Well, perhaps you'd like to tell us about them."

Matron shook her head. "Maybe some other time," she said, sounding a little embarrassed.

They all smiled.

It was now time for the treasure hunt to begin in earnest. Henry had already started, and was dashing up and down the beach, barking at nothing in particular, his tail wagging like the pendulum of a clock that has gone out of control. Now and then he stopped and dug furiously in the sand with his front paws, before losing interest and moving on to another spot.

"Look at Henry," said Tanya. "He must know why we're here."

Ben disagreed. "I doubt it," he said. "He just likes digging."

But Badger thought that Henry might be on to something. "Dogs smell things we can't," he pointed out. "Henry might be able to sniff out treasure. Who knows?"

"More likely an old bone," Fee suggested. "Dogs only think of their stomachs."

"We'll see," said Miss Worsfold. "He's having a great time, anyway. And the exercise will do him good."

Miss Worsfold clapped her hands together. "Right then, everybody," she called out. "Time to get going."

They gathered around the teacher and listened carefully to her instructions. Tanya and Poppy would take it in turns with the metal detector to sweep the ground at the top of the beach. "The Vikings wouldn't bury their treasure in the sand itself," she said, "because it might get washed away by the tide. And of course the wind can easily change the shape of a sand dune dramatically. The worst thing for anybody burying something on a beach, I should imagine, would be to come back and not be able to recognise the place they'd put it.

"While Tanya and Poppy are working here," she continued, "the others will split into two groups. One group – that's you, Fee, Thomas and Matron – will go and explore the river. Ben and Badger will search further along the shore to see if there are any caves. Poppy and Ben, you told the Captain you thought that a cave would be a likely place to hide treasure, didn't you? I'll stay here with Henry and help with the metal detector."

She paused. "And we'll meet up at the top of the hill by the waterfall in an hour," she said, pointing to the hill a little way back from the beach. "Any questions?"

Nobody wanted to waste any time, so Miss Worsfold showed Tanya and Poppy how to use the metal detector. That did not take long. All they had to do, it seemed, was to put on earphones, move the switch to the *on* position, and then sweep the instrument in front of them as they walked.

"Don't do it too quickly," warned Miss Worsfold. "You don't want to miss anything. And if it beeps at you, then there's metal down below. Start digging. But don't get too excited," she cautioned. "Just because it beeps doesn't mean there's treasure. It might only be that you've found an old belt buckle."

While Fee and Thomas set off to explore the banks of the river with Matron, Ben and Badger went in the opposite direction to search for caves, a task that took them off along the rocky shore beyond the mouth of the river.

It was a warm day and the sky was completely clear. High up above them, they saw a pair of sea eagles, circling effortlessly. Even at that height, the birds' great wing span made them clearly visible from the ground.

"Look at them," said Badger, pointing. "That would be a great place to search from. You'd see everything laid out below you."

Ben gazed upwards. "And they can spot the tiniest detail," he said. "Their eyesight is amazing."

As they watched, one of the eagles suddenly swooped down like an arrow, its wings tucked in tight. They did not see exactly where it went, as its target was beyond a small rise along the shore. But when it rose up again, above the level of the trees, they saw that it was clutching a large fish in its talons.

The two boys looked at one another. It had been such a remarkable thing to witness, and it had a chilling effect on them. Neither said anything, but they were both thinking the same thing. This was a wild and untamed place where anything could happen. What if somebody was watching them – just as closely as that eagle had been watching its prey before striking it with such deadly precision?

Ben tried not to think about it and remarked how the shore had just the right sort of rock for the formation of caves.

And they did find a cave. A few minutes later, as they scrambled over a group of large rocks, they saw before them a sizeable dark mouth in the rock. The tide was half in, half out, and this had exposed the entrance to the cave. At high tide, Ben thought, it would be largely underwater.

They stood at the entrance and peered inside. Although there was bright sunlight outside, it was dark inside and difficult to see beyond the first few rocks.

"Just as well we brought a flashlight," said Badger.

"I know," agreed Ben. "It would be impossible to see how deep the cave is without it."

They began to explore the cave. Its floor was sand, still moist from the last high tide. There were small outcrops of rock, covered in barnacles, the tiny shells

Oars: necessary if anything went wrong with the motor

Coils of rope

Spade

Life-jackets

Outboard engine: fuelled and clamped into position

A metal detector ... the one thing that, more than anything else, would be useful on a treasure-hunting expedition.

Although there was bright sunlight outside, it was dark inside and difficult to see beyond the first few rocks.

dotting the dark surface with white. There were mussels too, clinging to the rock amid tangled growths of dark seaweed.

They made their way further into the cave, clambering over slippery boulders, being careful not to tread in the occasional pool of seawater. Then the cave came to an end with a face of flat rock, rising up to a roof that they could barely make out in the darkness, even with the help of the flashlight.

Badger looked around. "Nothing here," he said, sounding disappointed.

Ben reluctantly agreed. He had hoped so much that they might find an old chest, tucked away behind a rock and forgotten all those centuries ago, but there was nothing. "Oh, well," he said. "Perhaps the others will be having more luck."

Together they made their way out of the cave, their eyes taking a while to adjust to the bright sunlight outside. Then they headed back the way they had come to give the others their disappointing news. If there was treasure to be found – and both Ben and Badger were now reluctantly reaching the conclusion that there might not be – it must be somewhere else.

Poppy, Tanya and Miss Worsfold were having no better luck with the metal detector. They had taken it in turns to wear the headphones and walk backwards and forwards over the rough, broken ground. It was slow going, as they had to make their way round large clumps of heather and thick clusters of gorse bushes.

"Nothing," said Poppy, as she handed the metal detector over to Tanya. "Not even the slightest squeak."

Tanya's results were the same, although Miss Worsfold, when it was her turn, did find a piece of rusty chain. This caused brief excitement, only to be followed by disappointment. "It's probably just part of an old anchor chain. Certainly nothing to do with the Vikings," she said.

Meanwhile, Fee and Thomas, accompanied by Matron, had been following the river upstream, looking out for likely spots where the Vikings might have hidden their treasure. There were one or two places that looked promising, but which, on closer investigation, revealed nothing. After a while, they decided to give up and head up to the waterfall, where they were all due to meet.

Matron sighed. "I'm afraid this has been very much a wild goose chase."

Neither Fee nor Thomas felt they could disagree.

"Oh well," said Thomas. "At least it's been interesting."

Matron said that she thought so too.

A moment later they rounded a corner, and there

was the waterfall. They had heard it from some distance away, but now it was straight in front of them – a solid wall of dark, peaty water cascading down to a large pool at its base, throwing up plumes of white spray that was caught by the wind.

They stopped and stared in wonder.

"Look at that!" exclaimed Matron. "What a drop!"

Fee had to struggle to make her voice heard above the roar of the water. "It's very high," she said.

Matron looked up. There was a glint in her eye. "It would be wonderful to dive from up there," she said. "Straight into that pool down below."

"But it's far too high," Thomas protested.

"Not for me!" said Matron.

A deadly dive

Just as Matron said this, Poppy, Tanya, Miss Worsfold and Henry arrived, and reported that their search, too, had been unsuccessful. "We looked everywhere," said Tanya, "but apart from an old anchor chain there was nothing."

"Perhaps there never was any treasure," said Miss Worsfold. "Or perhaps somebody found it a long time ago."

Matron shrugged. She always looked on the bright side and saw no reason to be too disappointed about treasure that might never even have existed. "Oh, well," she said. "No matter: we've all had a very enjoyable time exploring." She looked at her watch. "And I think it's just about time for our picnic. Where on earth have Ben and Badger got to? We'll just have to start without them!"

Thomas was pleased about the picnic. He had been too excited to eat much at breakfast, and was now beginning to feel pangs of hunger.

Miss Worsfold walked off to look at the pool beneath the waterfall as the others unpacked the food. Here the river whirled about before resuming its course down to the shore of the sea loch. She bent down and cautiously dipped a finger into the water.

"This water's warmer than you'd think," she called out. "I suppose the sun heats it up."

Matron joined her at the water's edge. "I was thinking of taking a dip," she said. "I have my swimming costume on underneath already. You never know when you might get the chance to swim – or dive."

With the mention of diving, Miss Worsfold glanced up towards the top of the waterfall. "From up there?" she asked anxiously.

Matron smiled. "There's a narrow shelf of rock just below the top," she said. "Can you see it? It would be a good diving platform."

Miss Worsfold shielded her eyes against the sun. "Yes, I see it." She sounded hesitant. "But are you sure it's not too high?"

Matron did not answer. She was already peeling off her jacket.

"Come on, Matron!" shouted Thomas. "Let's see one of your famous dives."

Thomas knew, as did everybody, that Matron had once been an Olympic diver. Most of the people on the *Tobermory* had seen her diving from the side of the ship, or sometimes higher up, from one of the spars – the horizontal beams from which the sails are hung. They were always impressed by the elegance and daring of her diving, and the way she entered the water so cleanly, with barely a splash.

Matron smiled. "If you really want me to," she said.

"We do," urged Fee.

Matron looked carefully at the pool. Away from the waterfall, where the water was calm, it was possible to see the sand at the bottom – a yellow expanse, marked by rippling shadows from the surface. As an experienced diver, Matron knew that you must never dive into water without knowing exactly how deep it is. If it is too shallow you risk serious injury.

"It looks deep enough," said Thomas, who had gone to stand beside Matron.

"Yes," she agreed. "It's fine for diving."

They watched as Matron began to make the steep ascent to the narrow platform of rock. It was a tricky climb, as the stone underfoot was wet and slippery with spray from the waterfall. Halfway up, Matron stopped to take a rest. She waved to everybody down below.

It was just at this moment that Ben and Badger came into view. They had decided to explore a little further, and their route had taken them across the side of a hill near the waterfall. Looking down, the two boys saw their friends sitting at the edge of the pool, and Matron too, who, after a brief rest, had resumed her climb.

"What's going on, Badger?" asked Ben. "Isn't that Matron climbing up the side of the waterfall?"

Badger screwed up his eyes to see more clearly. "I think so," he said. "And it looks like she's wearing her swimming costume."

"That's odd," Ben remarked. "Why would she go up there in her swimming costume?"

The answer came to him almost immediately. "Of course! You know Matron loves to dive, Badger," he said, just as he noticed something that made his heart miss a beat. "Badger!" he gasped, grabbing his friend's arm. "Look over there! Look at the pool at the bottom of the waterfall."

Once he followed the other boy's gaze, Badger saw with horror what Ben was pointing out to him. In the pool, directly below the place from which Matron was planning to dive, was a thin needle of rock poking just a little way above the surface of the water. Because of the way the sunlight was glinting on the surface, Matron had not seen what was clearly visible from where Ben and Badger were watching.

She had now reached the shelf of rock and was peering down at the pool. Poppy, Fee, Tanya, Thomas and Miss Worsfold waved up to her from below.

Matron lifted her arms up in the air, preparing to launch herself into the void. Ben gasped. "Oh no! She hasn't seen the rock. She'll hit it, Badge. Matron will hit the rock! We have to do something!"

Ben and Badger's furious shouting and waving caught Matron's attention and she waved back smiling, responding to what she assumed was the two boys' friendly greeting, and then raised her arms again for the dive.

Immediately realising that she had misunderstood their warning, and without pausing to tell Ben what he was going to do, Badger ran as fast as he possibly could, and within a few moments had reached the pool at the foot of the waterfall. Cupping his hands together, he shouted at the top of his voice, "Matron! Matron! There's a rock! Don't dive!"

Matron saw Badger, but the roar of the waterfall drowned out his warning. Thinking that Badger was simply encouraging her, she waved enthusiastically back. Then she prepared once more to make her dive.

Badger now realised there was only one way in which he could stop the impending disaster. Without taking off his shoes or clothes, he jumped into the pool and began to swim as fast as he could towards the rock. Up above him, Matron looked down in puzzlement. What was Badger up to? Was he trying to spoil her dive? She could not dive with him immediately below her, as that would risk injury to both of them. She lowered her arms and gestured for Badger to get out of the way. But Badger stayed exactly where he was, treading water to keep himself afloat, looking up from time to time to try and catch her eye.

Matron was now extremely cross. Badger, she thought, was being deliberately obstructive. But why? Whatever the reason, she could not dive as long as he was there. She waited for a while to see if he would move, but when he did not, she reluctantly concluded that she would have to abandon the dive. It was most annoying, and she would certainly give him a piece of her mind when she got back to the side of the pool.

When Badger saw her climbing down, he struck out for the shore. He was keen to get out of the water, as his sodden clothes made swimming difficult and tiring.

"What on earth were you playing at?" Matron snapped at Badger a few minutes later. "I went all the way up there for nothing – thanks to you."

Badger shook himself to get some of the water out of his hair and clothes. "Didn't you see the rock?" he said, gasping for breath.

Matron frowned. "What rock?" she asked angrily.

Badger pointed to the place where he had been swimming. "Right there," he said. "Look, you can just see it from here, now the sun's shifted."

Matron looked where he was pointing. "I can't see any—" And then she stopped. With the direct sunlight off the surface of the water, she could now make out the sharp sliver of rock she had failed to notice before.

Matron's jaw dropped. "Oh ..." she muttered. "Oh, no." She looked at Badger with gratitude. "Badger, I think you saved my life," she said.

"I tried to warn you by shouting," said Badger. "But the waterfall drowned out my words."

"And I would have been badly hurt," said Matron, "if it hadn't been for you."

Miss Worsfold had now come across and was anxious to know what was happening. "Well done, Badger," she said, when she realised just how close Matron had come to injuring herself – or worse. "That was quick thinking on your part. The Captain will be very impressed when we tell him what you did."

Badger was now shivering from the cold, his clothes sticking to his skin uncomfortably. Fortunately, since everybody had brought a change of clothing, he was soon out of his sodden garments and dressed in a new dry outfit. Then, together with Ben, he went over to join the others.

"I think you deserve the last piece of cake for that," said Matron. "That's the least I can do to thank you."

Badger told her that that was not really necessary,

but accepted nonetheless. He had a weakness for chocolate, and the piece of cake that Matron was offering him was covered in thick chocolate icing.

Fee watched him enviously. She shared Badger's taste for chocolate, and she would dearly have loved a taste of the large slice he was now holding.

Badger noticed. "Do you like chocolate cake, Fee?" he said, dwelling on the words *chocolate* and *cake*.

Fee struggled to conceal her longing. "I don't mind it," she said, trying to sound as if she wasn't bothered in the slightest if she never had chocolate cake again.

Badger laughed. Then, breaking the piece of cake into two, he offered the larger piece to Fee.

"Oh, I can't," said Fee. "That was your reward from Matron."

"Go on," Badger urged her. "I want you to have it."

Fee gave in, and thanked him as she took a bite of the delicious cake. Ben watched and thought to himself, *This is my old friend well and truly back. This is the Badger I've always liked so much.*

Whilst everyone was finishing the picnic, Henry had been sniffing around for any unwanted morsels. Matron had already given him a couple of dog biscuits, which he wolfed down in seconds, and he had also found half a sausage roll that Thomas had inadvertently dropped. Finding nothing else, he decided to do a bit of exploring. There were all sorts of things to be investigated, and of course there was that strange cascade of falling water – Henry had never seen a waterfall before and was eager to find out what it was and why it made that roaring sound.

Trotting round the other side of the pool, pausing now and then to sniff at this and that, Henry soon found himself on a narrow pathway of rock stretching all the way to the foot of the waterfall. At the end of the path the water hit the surface with a great roar, throwing up a huge cloud of spray. Jumping across some rocks at the side of the waterfall, Henry picked his way through the spray, curious as to what lay behind.

Now, completely hidden from the other side, Henry found himself in a sort of cavern which stretched far back into the darkness. Keen to explore further, and not at all bothered by the cold and lack of light, he trotted deeper into the gloom. In the furthest corner he came upon a pile of strange objects, all covered with mud and slime. He sniffed at them. They had what seemed to him a very old smell – a smell he had never encountered before. But since they didn't appear to be edible, there was nothing much to interest him, and he trotted back towards the waterfall.

Ben had been watching Henry as he made his way round the side of the pool. When the dog disappeared behind the waterfall, he started to feel worried, as he had no idea what might be beyond it. The pool might well extend behind, and its waters would be churning angrily with the force of the falling water. If that was so, Henry could be in real danger.

"Let's check up on Henry," Ben said to Badger. "I'm worried."

"Don't worry. He'll be all right," replied Badger, munching the rest of his slice of cake. "Dogs are good at taking care of themselves."

Ben was not convinced. "No," he insisted. "Let's go and take a look – just to be sure."

Badger agreed, rather reluctantly, and followed his friend round the path to the place where Henry had vanished from view.

The noise of the water was deafening, rather like that of an aeroplane or of the engine of an express train. Ben signalled to Badger to follow him. It would have been pointless to try to make himself heard, and together they clambered into the hidden chamber.

It was dark behind the waterfall, and it took some time before their eyes became accustomed to the lack of light. A friendly bark from Henry announced that he was safe and sound before they could actually see him in the gloom. When they began to see more clearly, they discovered that the chamber they were in was far bigger than they had imagined. Not only was it high – they could hardly see the stone roof above them in the semi-darkness – but it also stretched back some distance into mysterious blackness.

"It goes back a long way," said Ben, taking his flashlight out of his pocket. He shone it towards the back of the cave, but its beam just disappeared in the gloom.

"Shall we go and take a look?" asked Badger.

Ben swallowed hard. He would never have been brave enough to explore a cave like this alone, he thought, but it was different with Badger. Having a friend with you can help a great deal, so he gave his agreement. "Yes," he said. "Let's take a look. You never know what you'll find."

"Until you start looking for it," said Badger, laughing, before adding, "All right then, Henry, you lead the way!"

They made their way slowly across a jumble of small rocks that had fallen from the roof of the cave and were now cluttering the ground. Ben wondered what would happen if another rock were to fall while they were there, but he did not say anything about his fears. *Sometimes*, he thought, *it's best to say nothing* – and this was one of those times.

They were now deep inside the cave. Ben moved the beam of his flashlight across the damp stone walls. While he was doing that, something suddenly dropped down from above and fluttered past, causing both boys to jump with fright and Henry to give a short, high-pitched bark.

"A bat!" exclaimed Badger, once he had recovered from the shock.

They moved on and finally reached the back of the cave. "We can't go any further. We're at the end," said Ben. "Perhaps we should turn back."

"Yes," said Badger. "I think we've seen everything there is to see."

But then, just as he said that, the beam of Ben's flashlight fell on a pile of objects on the floor of the cave, right at the back. Stooping to investigate, Badger picked up one of them and showed it to Ben. As he did so a thick layer of dried mud fell away from the object and its true nature was revealed. Now they knew what they – or more accurately Henry – had discovered. This must be the Viking treasure that had been brought ashore from the sinking longboat and hidden behind the wall of water, and which had lain forgotten and undiscovered until now.

Badger was holding what seemed to be an old cup. After wiping it with his sleeve, he exposed the dull gleam of a golden goblet. Ben picked up a smaller object, and after some vigorous rubbing revealed an intricate piece of jewellery – a brooch in the shape of a wild boar.

"Viking treasure!" shouted Ben "We've found the treasure, Badge!"

Matron lifted her arms
up in the air, preparing
to launch herself
into the void.

This must be the
Viking treasure
that had been
brought ashore ...

Accompanied by Henry, who had by now had quite enough of waterfalls and caverns, the two friends returned as quickly as they could to the others. Miss Worsfold, clapped her hands in sheer delight at the thought that they had finally found the ancient treasure.

Ben explained that there were far too many things in the cave for them to be able to carry safely back in one journey. Miss Worsfold listened carefully and suggested that they should take the goblet and the brooch back to the *Tobermory* to show the Captain, and return to collect everything else. "Some of these items will be very fragile by now after lying there for so long," she said. "We shall need to be careful with them."

Without wasting any time, the whole party made its way back to the beach.

"Right," said Miss Worsfold. "Everyone lend a hand to launch the boat."

It was then that Ben noticed something odd.

"Look! There's only one oar," he exclaimed. "What's happened to the other?"

Just as he spoke, Poppy spotted something else.

"And somebody's taken the propeller off the outboard engine," she said, pointing to the place where the propeller ought to be.

"Oh, no," groaned Ben. "How are we going to get back with only one oar and no engine?"

That same question was also in the mind of a group of people looking down at them from the ridge of the hill above the waterfall. One of them was watching closely through binoculars.

"Our young friends have just got back to their boat," he said with a cruel laugh. "I think they've realised they're going to be stuck there for a good long time."

"Yes," said one of the others, a tall, thin man with a shaggy beard. "And they don't even know we're here. What a stroke of luck we spotted them down by the pool, just as we were on the point of giving up. Now, whilst they're figuring out what to do, let's go down to the cave, find what we've been looking for and get back to the *Swordfish*."

How incredibly lucky, thought the man with the beard again, that two foolish boys, and one equally foolish dog, had unwittingly led them straight to the Viking treasure.

CHAPTER 13

The chase is on!

Miss Worsfold took her phone out of her pocket. "I'll speak to the Captain," she announced. "He'll send another boat over to tow us back to the *Tobermory*."

This was the simplest solution to the situation in which they had suddenly found themselves. But as she switched on her phone and prepared to key in the Captain's number, her face fell.

Poppy, who was watching closely, guessed immediately what the problem was. "No signal?" she asked.

Miss Worsfold nodded. "I'm afraid not. It's the mountains, I think. They're blocking it."

With that possibility closed to them, rescue was very unlikely – at least not until someone on board the *Tobermory* realised they were missing and sent a boat to look for them. But that might not be for hours.

As they stood there without a clue as to what to do next, Poppy started to think about who might have sabotaged their boat. "I bet it was the crew of the *Swordfish*," she said. "Maybe they had the same idea as us and thought the treasure might be hidden on land somewhere near here."

Miss Worsfold nodded. "I can't see anyone else around," she said. "But you could well be right, Poppy."

"But why would they want to stop us from leaving?" asked Tanya.

"They might have seen us," Badger said. "They might have been watching when Ben and I went behind the waterfall and came back with the goblet and brooch."

"And then one of them could have run back down here and done this to our boat," added Fee. "They guessed we would go straight back to the *Tobermory* to get help to shift the treasure. But now we're stuck here."

Miss Worsfold agreed that this was quite possible. "If that's true," she said, "then this is a serious situation and we must to get back to the *Tobermory* as soon as we possibly can. We need help before it's too late. But how are we going to get there now?"

Suddenly, Ben had an idea. "The tide's going out, isn't it?"

"Yes," said Miss Worsfold. "You can see it. There's quite a strong current here."

Ben glanced at the narrows, where the water

drained out into the main part of Loch Sunart.

"Miss Worsfold," he began, "if we push our boat out into the water, won't it be carried by the tide?"

"I suppose so," said Miss Worsfold. "But don't forget: we have only one oar and no outboard engine. We would be at the mercy of the current."

Badger saw what Ben was driving at. "Yes!" he shouted. "Yes, Ben. That's it! We'd be carried out through the narrows straight towards the *Tobermory*. They'd soon see us and come to help us."

Miss Worsfold looked doubtful at first, but then she smiled. "I think it could be worth trying," she said. And then, after thinking about it more, she added, "Yes, I think that's by far the best plan. Well done, Ben. And Badger too. Good thinking."

The tide was now moving much more rapidly, and once they had pushed the boat out from the shore it was quickly caught by the current. The single oar they had left proved useful as a rudder. By lowering its blade into the water behind them, Ben and Badger were able to steer the boat – but it was hard work in such a strong current. As they approached the narrows, where the current ran at its fastest, they struggled with the oar, just managing to keep clear of the jagged rocks on either side of the passage. But then they were through, and everybody gave a cheer when the boat at last drifted out into calm open water.

"We've done it!" shouted Tanya.

"Look, there's the *Tobermory*," Poppy yelled. Henry, just as excited and relieved as the others, added a few barks to the clamour. Miss Worsfold, though, was beginning to feel anxious. "I hope they see us," she said. There was a danger, she thought, that they might not and they could end up drifting out to sea. That would be serious, as a small boat like theirs, especially with no outboard and just one oar, could very easily be swamped by the first large wave it encountered.

Fortunately, Miss Worsfold's fears proved unfounded. No sooner had they made it through the narrows than Amanda Birtwhistle, who happened to be on the deck of the *Tobermory* at the time, spotted them. Quickly fetching a pair of binoculars, she trained them on the boat. She instantly recognised Miss Worsfold at the bow and Ben and Badger at the stern. And Henry's head, leaning over the side.

Amanda made her way down to the Captain's cabin to tell him what she had seen. He was soon on deck with Mr Rigger, who gave the order to lower one of the small boats.

"It looks like they need a tow," said Mr Rigger as he summoned Rory Quinn to lend a hand. Rory fetched a strong rope from a locker and then the two of them set off on their rescue mission.

Ben was the first to see them approaching. Standing up in the boat, he waved his arms energetically crossways in the distress signal that is always recognised at sea. From the other boat, Rory waved back.

"They'll be here in no time," said Matron, with relief. She was not very fond of small boats and was keen to be back on board the *Tobermory* as soon as possible.

A line was thrown from boat to boat and safely secured. Then, with the engine of the rescue boat straining at the task, they made their way slowly back to the safety of the *Tobermory*. Captain Macbeth was there to welcome them as they climbed back up the gangway that had been lowered for their return.

"Come down to my cabin straight away," he said. "Mr Rigger and I would like to know exactly what happened."

Once inside, Miss Worsfold did most of the talking, although she left it to Ben and Badger to relate what had happened behind the waterfall. "It was really Henry who found the treasure," said Ben. "He deserves the credit."

The Captain smiled. "I'm sure Cook will make him a fine dinner as a reward," he said, but his smile faded when Miss Worsfold told him how they thought their boat had been sabotaged by the crew of the *Swordfish*.

"Yes, I noticed the *Swordfish* at anchor near the

entrance to the narrows, and there's no sign of anyone on board. I think we'd better get back to that cave soon as possible," he said. "Those people are definitely up to no good."

Mr Rigger agreed. "I'll find some large sacks," he said. "Cook usually has some. We can use them to carry the treasure back."

"I'll come myself," said Captain Macbeth. "And Mr Rigger." He looked at Ben, and then at Badger. "And you two, I think – to show us the way."

"And Henry," Badger suggested.

"Yes," said the Captain. "I think Henry deserves to come too."

Half an hour later, the boat carrying the Captain, Mr Rigger, Ben, Badger – and Henry – nosed away from the side of the *Tobermory* and headed back towards the narrows. It was slack tide now, the point at which the tide is neither going out nor coming in, and so there was no current to hinder their progress. Soon they had negotiated their way through the narrows, and the beach and river mouth were in sight.

"Captain!" Ben said, tugging urgently at Captain Macbeth's sleeve. "Look – there's a boat."

"And some people," Mr Rigger added. "It looks as if they're loading something."

Captain Macbeth stopped the engine. "I'll take a closer look," he said, raising his binoculars.

They waited in silence while he assessed the situation. They did not have long to wait, though, as he soon lowered the binoculars and handed them to Mr Rigger. "What do you think, Mr Rigger?" he asked.

Mr Rigger took the binoculars. When he had finished with them, his expression was grim. "Gold," he said. "They're loading gold objects into the boat."

"Just as I feared," Captain Macbeth said. "We'll have to try and stop them."

Without delay, the Captain opened the throttle of the outboard engine and the boat pushed forcefully through the water, creating a widening white wake behind it. On the shore, the four men hauling the Viking treasure onto their boat looked up, alerted by the noise of the engine. They had just loaded the last of the items, and lost no time in leaping into the boat and starting the outboard. Theirs was a much more powerful engine and it propelled their vessel through the water at a speed that Captain Macbeth could never manage.

It was an unequal contest, and it soon became clear that there was no chance of stopping the *Swordfish* crew from getting back to their boat with the treasure and rapidly hauling up their anchor. By the time Captain Macbeth's boat had made it back through the narrows, the *Swordfish* was already on the move and heading out towards the open sea.

Realising that there was no point in continuing the chase, Captain Macbeth turned his boat back towards the *Tobermory*.

Ben and Badger watched in dismay. They had been thrilled at finding Viking treasure, but now they felt only intense disappointment. It had lain hidden for so long, and now, just when it was within their grasp, it had been snatched from under their very noses.

By the time they reached the *Tobermory* they had given up all hope. Unless they left their anchorage within a matter of minutes, the *Swordfish* would soon be well beyond their reach and the treasure would be gone forever.

But Captain Macbeth was not yet ready to give up. "All hands on deck! All hands on deck!" he boomed over the public address system. "We set sail as soon as possible. And Mr Rigger, please radio the coastguard and tell them there's a boat making off with Viking treasure!"

The crew had practised emergency departure many times, and now, doing it for real, they went through all the steps with ease. In record time the great anchor was raised and safely secured, loose items lashed down or stowed, and the main sails freed from their bindings. Then, with Captain Macbeth at the helm, the ship turned its bow in the direction of the fleeing *Swordfish*. The chase was on.

Ben and Badger were working the sails, winding in the sheets – the lines used to make the foresails drumskin-tight to the wind. It was a hard task, but they enjoyed working together and they made a good team. Poppy and Fee were on helming duty with Captain Macbeth, responding to his shouted instructions to adjust their course by five degrees here and ten degrees there. Up on the main mast, perched in the crow's nest, Rory and Tanya kept a lookout for the *Swordfish* and shouted to the Captain down below when they sighted their target.

The *Tobermory* carried more sail than the *Swordfish*. This gave them an advantage when it came to speed, and that, together with expert sailing on the young crew's part, meant that they gradually gained on the other ship. That caused alarm on the *Swordfish*, whose crew could be seen running around the deck desperately trying to coax their sails into giving them an extra turn of speed. They did not succeed, though, and slowly but surely the *Tobermory* got closer and closer.

It was then that the captain of the *Swordfish* made his decision. He had realised that he would not be able to get away, and if he were stopped – as seemed certain now – he would be caught red-handed with stolen treasure on board.

With a worried look on his face, he ordered his men to turn the boat into the wind. This meant the vessel immediately slowed down, coming to a halt some way off a bay fringed by a wide beach.

Watching from the deck of the *Tobermory*, Badger asked Ben what he thought the other ship was doing. But before Ben could say anything, the answer became clear. On the deck of the *Swordfish* the crew could be seen carrying sacks up from down below and tossing them into the water.

"Oh no," groaned Ben. "They're throwing the treasure into the water."

Captain Macbeth had noticed this too, and he shouted out in anger. "Oh, you can't do that!" he yelled, shaking his fists at the same time. "Stop, you villains! Stop!"

Of course the crew of the *Swordfish* paid no attention to this, and soon every sack of treasure had been dumped overboard. And then the *Swordfish* turned sharply, picking up the wind once more, and sped off.

Poppy was standing on deck near Captain Macbeth and Mr Rigger as they surveyed the scene, listening to their debate.

"We must go after them," said Mr Rigger. "We can't let them get away. We have to keep on their tail until the coastguard gets here."

Captain Macbeth frowned. "But if we chase them, we'll never find the treasure again. It will be carried out into the depths by the current."

"But if we stay to get the treasure," said Mr Rigger, "they'll get clean away."

It was a very difficult decision for Captain Macbeth to take. If they chased the *Swordfish*, they lost the treasure; if they stayed to recover the treasure, they lost the *Swordfish*. For a few moments he hesitated, uncertain as to what to do. Then Poppy made her suggestion.

"Why not do both?" she asked. "We can send a small boat with divers to get the treasure. They can bring it up while we chase after the *Swordfish*. Then the *Tobermory* can come back for the divers."

Captain Macbeth stroked his beard. "I think that just might be a very good idea, Poppy," he said. Then, without wasting any more time, he ordered the *Tobermory* to turn round so that they could go to the place where they had seen the treasure being thrown overboard. As the *Tobermory* cut through the water, her sails billowing in the wind, Matron and Miss Worsfold were kitted out in diving gear. A boat was put over the side to be rowed by Tanya and Thomas to take the divers to where the treasure had entered the water.

Once the dive boat had been dispatched, the *Tobermory* set out after the *Swordfish*, using every ounce of speed the Captain could muster. The *Swordfish* had a start on them, of course, but once again the superior sailing skill of the *Tobermory*'s crew, and the fact that she was a bigger ship, worked to their advantage.

Soon they had caught up with the other boat and Captain Macbeth was able to shout across the small distance that separated the two vessels. "You'll never get away!" he shouted. "The coastguard is on the way. You must surrender."

No sooner had he given them this message than Ben spotted the coastguard vessel, the *Dolphin*, approaching at great speed. "They're almost here," he shouted to the Captain.

Captain Macbeth ordered Poppy to the helm. "Don't get too close," he said to her. "Just stick on their tail."

Poppy was an expert at the helm, and she kept the *Tobermory* a constant distance from the *Swordfish*. It was tiring work, but it was not long before the *Dolphin*, cutting through the water like a knife through butter, came up behind them.

"We're going to board her!" shouted the captain of the *Dolphin*. "Stand by."

Everybody on the *Tobermory* watched in anticipation as the naval boat edged closer and closer to the *Swordfish*. And when the boarding party leapt onto the other ship's deck and took control, the *Tobermory* crew gave a loud cheer – everyone, that is, except Hardtack, Shark and Flubber, who had looked glum throughout the entire operation.

"Well done, everyone," said Captain Macbeth, pleased that his young crew had performed so well again. "Poppy, that was excellent helming," he added. "Now, Hardtack and Shark, come with me. And Flubber too – I can't believe you're not involved in this too, somehow. I'd like to know more about the crew of the *Swordfish* and how they came to know about the Viking treasure. I don't believe they found out about it all on their own."

The three boys followed the Captain down below, their heads bowed, as everyone else looked on. "In trouble again," murmured Fee as they shuffled past. *What will the punishment be this time?* she thought to herself. However harsh it was, they would still be given another chance. Captain Macbeth was reluctant to give up on people. But they would have to be very careful in future.

While the coastguard crew were on board the *Swordfish* making their arrest, Ben was standing at the rail with Rory Quinn, watching everything that was happening. Rory was very quiet and trembling slightly, and Ben asked him whether anything was wrong.

"Aren't you pleased they've been caught?" he asked.

Rory turned to him. He pointed mutely towards the other boat. It seemed to Ben that something was stopping him from speaking.

"Are you all right, Rory?" he asked, now very concerned about his friend.

It took a few moments for Rory to respond. Then he said, in a voice that was cracked with emotion, "It's him, Ben! It's him."

"Who?" asked Ben. "What are you talking about, Rory?"

Rory pointed towards the *Swordfish*. "Their captain," he stuttered. "It's him. The pirate."

It took Ben a few moments to work out what Rory meant, but then he understood. "You mean that's the man who got away after robbing your father's boat? The one who threatened to get even with you?"

Rory nodded. "Yes. It's him. It's definitely him."

Ben smiled. "Well, you won't have to worry about him any longer, Rory. He's safely under arrest now and will be spending a long time in prison, I imagine."

Rory stopped shaking. "It's a great relief," he said. "I've been frightened stiff for ages, Ben."

"No longer," said Ben, patting Rory on the shoulder. "Your nightmare's over, Rory."

That evening, Captain Macbeth addressed the whole school in the mess hall.

"You will all have seen what happened this afternoon," he began, "and I'm happy to report that the treasure will be handed over to the museum authorities, who even as I speak are on the way from Edinburgh specially to take possession of these important items."

This was the signal for everybody to clap. The Captain let the applause go on for a few seconds before he held up his hands to silence it. "I hope you're not applauding me," he said, "because I don't deserve the credit for this. That goes to the two boys who discovered the treasure."

There was more applause, as everyone turned towards Ben and Badger.

"And Henry too!" shouted Badger.

Everybody laughed, and all eyes fell on the Captain's dog, who lifted his head, uttered two barks and then curled up on the floor.

Later, when they were lying in their hammocks after lights out and the ship was rocking gently at anchor, Badger said to Ben, "You know, Ben, I don't think I'll ever have as good a friend as you."

Ben waited a few moments before replying. "And I don't think I'll ever have one as good as you."

"We're both lucky, then," said Badger.

"Yes," said Ben. "I think we are."

And they were also lucky, Ben thought, to be at school on the School Ship *Tobermory*. The Captain had announced that the next day they would set sail for the Isle of Skye, a short distance to the north, and from there they would make a voyage all the way round the coast of Scotland. They had miles to go – miles and miles – but every one of those miles would be spent in the company of friends, and that, as everybody knows, makes any journey all the more rewarding, and all the more fun.

The End

If you have enjoyed this book, why not read other School Ship *Tobermory* adventures? Here is an excerpt from *School Ship Tobermory*, the first book in the series.

In Scotland in early summer, daylight lingers until it is quite late. For this reason they had to wait some time before it was dark enough to set off. But finally the last glow of the sun disappeared and the sea and the sky were joined in the same velvet black. Now the only light to be seen from the deck of the *Tobermory* were the silver pin-points of stars and, here and there, bobbing on the waves, the anchoring lights of boats in the bay.

"That's her," whispered Matron, pointing to a group of lights not far away. "That's their bow light up there; that's their stern light, and that's their mast. I can't see any other lights, which means they've all gone off to bed. They'll all be in their cabins."

"Just as well," said Poppy.

Matron looked about her. They had all gathered on deck. "Is everybody here?" she asked.

"I think so," said Poppy.

"Right," said Matron, still keeping her voice lowered. "Now, is everybody still happy to come along? If any of you are having second thoughts, now's the time to say."

There was silence. Then a voice spoke up. "Would you mind if I stayed?"

Everybody turned to see who had spoken.

"You see," said Angela Singh, "I'm just a little bit scared of the dark. I always have been."

If Angela had been anxious that people would laugh or make fun of her, her worries were soon shown to be unfounded.

"That's all right, Angela," said Matron. "Lots of people don't like the dark. It's nothing to be ashamed of."

"No it isn't," said Ben, who was standing next to Angela. "Don't worry. Nobody minds."

Matron asked Angela if she would stay on deck and keep a lookout. "It'll be useful having somebody here," she said. "If there's any problem, then flash this." She handed her a small black torch.

Now everything was ready. Badger had clambered down the rope ladder to the liberty boat, and was ready to help people down to join him. Fee went first, followed by Poppy. Then came the other boys – Ben and Thomas – and finally Matron.

Matron waited until Ben and Badger were ready with the oars. Then she said "Cast off!" and the boat moved silently away from the side of the ship, the only sound being that of the oars dipping gently into the water.

"That's good, boys," Matron whispered. "Row firm and hard. In and out. That's the way."

It was no more than a few minutes before they saw the dark bulk of the *Albatross* towering over them. From down below it looked enormous, and they realised that it would not be easy to get on board. But then Ben spotted something beneath the bowsprit, the sturdy pole that projects out from the bow of a sailing ship.

"There's a net hanging under the prow," he whispered to Matron. "Over there. Look!"

"Well spotted," whispered Matron. "Row that way."

It was one of those nets that are sometimes suspended beneath the bow of ships to catch anybody who falls off. That can happen when people are attending to rigging and lose their hold, or perhaps trip up over an untied lace, or are not ready for the sudden lurch of the ship as it crests a wave. The net on this ship had sagged, and so by standing up in the rowing boat, they were able to get hold of it and pull themselves up. Soon they were all on the deck of the *Albatross*, their rowing boat safely tied to a handy railing.

"Follow me," said Matron, her lowered voice barely audible above the breeze that had blown up.

In single file they moved slowly along the deck to the companionway. This was where Ben and Thomas had gone down below earlier that day, shortly before being stopped by Hardtack and Shark. Ben felt his breath coming quickly, almost in gasps. Fear had that effect on him, and he was now afraid, in spite of trying to be as brave as possible.

He was not alone. Keeping close to Poppy, Fee wondered what would happen if they were caught. If these people really were criminals, as Ben had suggested, then they could do anything – perhaps even be violent. And for her part, Poppy, who always seemed confident and cheerful, found herself keeping as close as she could to Matron.

They crept down below, where they were in complete, inky darkness. Matron was using a torch, the beam of which she largely shielded with a cupped hand, allowing it to emit only a faint sliver of light. But this was enough to make out where they were going and what lay about them.

On the first deck below they found the chart room, where the ship's navigator would plot the boat's course. Then they found the radio room, with its transmitters and microphones, its dials and lights, some of which were still glowing in the dark.

Suddenly the radio cackled into life. "*Albatross, Albatross, Albatross*," a voice said. "This is Shore Station Alpha. Are you receiving me? Over."

They froze.

"This is *Albatross*," whispered Ben to Matron. "They want to speak to us."

"I know how to work a radio," said Thomas, stepping forward. "Should I answer it?"

Matron said yes, adding that Ben should help by making a crackling noise in the background. This would sound like radio interference and it would help to disguise Thomas's voice.

"Shore Station Alpha," said Thomas. "This is *Albatross*. Receiving you loud and clear. Over."

And while he said this, Ben cleared his throat in the background, making a noise that sounded like airwave static. "*Ggghhh*," went Ben. And then, "*Hgghsh ghrrgh*."

There was a brief silence at the other end before the next transmission came. "*Albatross*, this is Shore Station Alpha. You are not very clear – please speak slowly. Have you got what you came for? Over."

Thomas looked enquiringly at Matron.

"Say yes," whispered Matron.

Thomas relayed the message, speaking more slowly now and with less noise from Ben.

"*Albatross*," came the voice once more, "this is Shore Station Alpha. Pick up further consignment from us the day after tomorrow. Two more captured yesterday to add to what you have. Can you confirm please? Over."

Again Thomas looked to Matron for guidance. Again Matron told him to say yes.

There came a final transmission. "*Albatross*, this is Shore Station Alpha. Filming deception worked. All local papers carried reports. Coast Guard not suspicious. No interest from police. Well done. Out."

Thomas put down the microphone.

They looked at one another and then at Matron, waiting to see if she could throw light on what they had just heard.

"This means only one thing," she said. "There is something on board this ship that they don't want anybody – particularly the Coast Guard – to know about."

"But what was that about two more being captured?" asked Poppy. "Two more what? People?"

Matron frowned. "I don't think so," she said. "Why would they be capturing people?"

Poppy shrugged. "Perhaps they're not after people; perhaps they're talking about something else altogether."

Matron pointed to the companionway that led to the lower decks. "Whatever it is will be down there," she said.

"Follow me."

She was about to leave the radio room when Fee, who was standing nearest to the door, heard a voice somewhere not far off. She tapped Matron's shoulder. "Somebody's coming," she whispered.

I

SCHOOL SHIP TOBERMORY

Ben and Fee MacTavish are off to a new school. But this is no ordinary school – it's the School Ship *Tobermory*, where young people from around the world train to be sailors and learn about all things nautical. When a film crew unexpectedly arrives, Ben is one of the lucky ones to be chosen as a movie extra. But his suspicions are soon aroused – are the director and his crew really making a film, or are they up to something sinister? Ben, Fee and their friends decide to investigate.

ISBN: 978 178027 343 3
£6.99

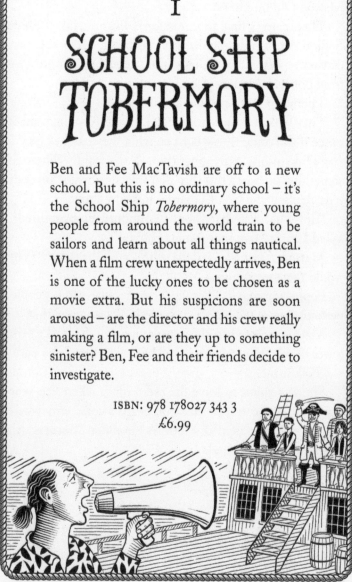

2

THE SANDS OF SHARK ISLAND

The crew of the School Ship *Tobermory* sets off for the Caribbean to explore some of the world's finest waters for sailing. Their routine of seamanship and snorkelling, kitesurfing and diving is soon interrupted, however, after Captain Macbeth comes into possession of an old map. When the map is stolen, Ben, Fee and their friends find themselves drawn into a mystery which leads them towards the sinister Shark Island.

ISBN: 978 1 78027 441 6
£6.99

3
THE RACE TO KANGAROO CLIFF

The School Ship *Tobermory* and its young crew
head down under to Australia for a Tall Ships
race. But a detour to rescue a boy
stranded on a small island leads to
further adventures when Henry,
Captain Macbeth's dog, disappears.
As the trail leads Ben and Fee
MacTavish and their intrepid
friends deeper into the bush,
they discover that a missing dog
is the least of their problems.

ISBN: 978 1 78027 453 9
£6.99